POCAHONTAS

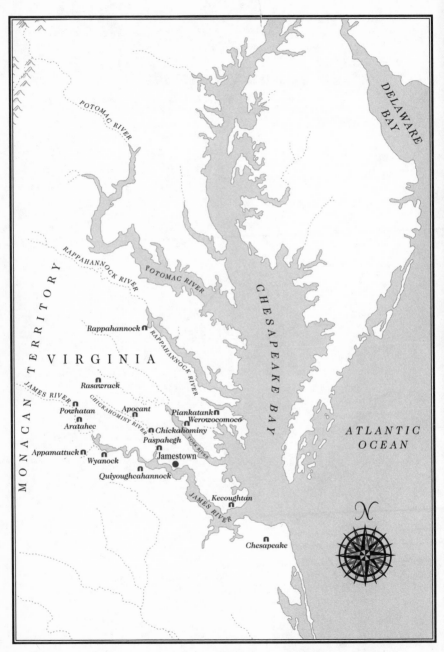

POCAHONTAS

Joseph Bruchac

SILVER WHISTLE
HARCOURT, INC.

Orlando ◆ *Austin* ◆ *New York* ◆ *San Diego* ◆ *Toronto* ◆ *London*

www.HarcourtBooks.com

Silver Whistle is a trademark of Harcourt, Inc., registered in
the United States of America and/or other jurisdictions.

Library of Congress Cataloging-in-Publication Data
Bruchac, Joseph, 1942–
Pocahontas/Joseph Bruchac.
p. cm.
"Silver Whistle."
Summary: Told from the viewpoints of Pocahontas and John Smith,
describes their lives in the context of the encounter between the Powhatan
Indians and the English colonists of 17th century Jamestown, Virginia.
1. Pocahontas, d. 1617—Juvenile literature. 2. Powhatan Indians—
Juvenile literature. 3. Smith, John, 1580–1531—Juvenile literature.
4. Virginia—History—Colonial period, ca. 1600–1775—Juvenile literature.
5. Jamestown (Va.)—History—Juvenile literature. [1. Pocahontas, c. 1617.
2. Powhatan Indians. 3. Smith, John, 1580–1531.
4. Jamestown (Va.)—History.] I. Title.
E99.P85B78 2003
975.5'01'092—dc21   2002007214
ISBN 0-15-216737-4

Text set in Adobe Caslon
Designed by Ivan Holmes

First edition
A C E G H F D B
Printed in Singapore

To Paula Wiseman, friend and editor, without whose encouragement this book never would have been written

You brave, heroic minds,
Worthy your country's name.
That honor still pursue,
Go and subdue,
Whilst loit'ring hinds
Lurk here at home with shame.

Britons, you stay too long;
Quickly aboard bestow you,
And with a merry gale
Swell your stretch'd sail,
With vows as strong
As the winds that blow you.

Your course securely steer,
West and by south forth keep;
Rocks, lee shores, nor shoals,
When Aeolus scowls,
You need not fear,
So absolute the deep.

And cheerfully at sea,
Success you still entice
To get the pearl and gold
And, ours to hold,
Virginia,
Earth's only paradise!

MICHAEL DRAYTON
FROM "ODE TO THE VIRGINIAN VOYAGE" CIRCA 1608

Contents

Preface

In December of 1607, a meeting took place between two very different people. Their cultures and languages, their views of the world, differed so greatly that understanding each other was close to impossible.

Yet communication did take place and, for a time, bonds of peace were forged between their two nations. The dramatic meeting of those two, an energetic eleven-year-old girl of the Powhatan nation and a twenty-seven-year-old Englishman whose intellect had been deepened and whose resolve had been hardened by his experiences as a warrior, would become one of the most powerful, romantic, and frequently told stories of American history. As a result of their legendary encounter, seeds were sown that grew into a new nation. This is the story of the events throughout the year of 1607 that led to that dramatic moment, the story of Pocahontas and John Smith.

1

POCAHONTAS

The Swan Canoes

*Long ago, Ahone, the Great Mysterious Spirit, created the
world. Great Ahone created Moon and Stars to brighten the
darkness of the night and to be companions and dwell with
Great Ahone.*

*Sun was also made by Great Ahone to give brightness and
warmth to the days. With that light of the Sun, all could be
seen, and all that had been made by Ahone was good to see.*

CATTAPEUK
TIME OF LEAVES RETURNING
LATE APRIL 1607

I AM MY FATHER'S favorite daughter. This means a great
deal, for he is Mamanatowic, the Great Chief of all the
Powhatan towns. My formal name is Amonute. But my everyday name is Pocahontas. That name, which almost everyone
calls me, fits my personality much better. In the language of the
Coatmen it might be translated as One Who Makes Mischief.
My father suggests that it really means She Who Wants to
Know Everything. He says that although I have only seen the
leaves return eleven times, I have already asked more questions
than most people do in a whole lifetime.

It is because I ask so many questions that, even though I was not there, I know what it was like in times past when the great swan canoes swam into sight on Chesepiock, our great salt bay. The man of Kecoughtan who first saw them said that for a few heartbeats—and his heart was beating very fast—he did not recognize what they were. Those *quintansuk* looked like birds, giant swans with huge white wings, breathing smoke and fire out of their beaks. When he realized what they were and who they must be carrying, his heartbeat became even faster. Tassantassuk. Outsiders! He quickly turned his *quintans*, made from the trunk of a cypress tree, and paddled as fast as he could to shore. He had to warn the people. The Tassantassuk had returned! They had come from the sunrise to our lands and waters before. Our memories of them were not good.

I am too young to have my own memories of the first arrival of the Outsiders. But my father's memory and the memories of our elders all look much further back along the circle of seasons than my eyes can see. It would be better if they were the ones to speak of what happened, but I will do my best to tell their memories truthfully.

The first Outsiders to come in such giant canoes called themselves Espaniuk. Some wondered if they were really men and not giant squirrels dressed in long coats. The faces of those coat-wearing men were as red and furry as squirrels. They also had long, clever fingers like those of Arakun, the masked one who scratches with his hands. Further, the Coatmen spoke in a strange language, which sounded to some of us like the growls and whines and barks of animals. Strange as they were, our people greeted and welcomed them as friends. That friendship did not last long. Those first Coatmen treated our people badly. When we protested the way they pushed us about, they attacked us.

Some of the Coatmen had what we thought to be hard shells like Terrapin, the Sea Turtle. Those shells were so hard that arrows and spears could not pierce them. The men also carried sticks that burned and then roared like thunder. Whenever the thunder sticks roared, they shot out a hail of small stones that made terrible wounds when they struck a person.

When our men finally caught one of those hard-shelled Espaniuk during a battle and skinned him, they were surprised at how easily his shell came off. They realized then that it was only a hard kind of clothing. Those first Coatmen finally saw they could not make us do as they wished. They left our land and waters.

When those Outsiders left, they stole one of our people, a man named Young Deer, whose father was werowance of Paspahegh. They took him across the wide water to a great island called Kew-ba. Then they sailed even farther, to the place where all men have faces like furry animals. Ten winters passed before those Outsiders came back. With them was Young Deer, who now dressed as the Coatmen dressed, wearing a long black robe. They called him Ton Loo-wee. He looked much like them, but our people recognized him. Hair had not grown to cover his cheeks, and he still knew how to speak as we human beings do.

The Coatmen thought Young Deer had become one of them. He had not. He threw off his long black coat and rejoined his people. Some of those black-robed Coatmen followed him to his uncle's home. They insulted Young Deer and tried to beat him. They called our people thieves because we picked up and took some of the things the Black Robes left lying about. Those black-robed Coatmen behaved so badly that all but one of them were killed. Some of our people thought that this ended the trouble. Young Deer told them otherwise.

"You do not know the Espaniuk as I do," he said. "More will come again from the sunrise in their great swan canoes. When they come, they will try to kill us."

Six moons passed, and it happened just as Young Deer had said. When the Corn Moon came, the Espaniuk returned. They killed many of our people with their thunder sticks. Then, once again, they left our land and waters. From that day on, the people of Paspahegh held both fear and hatred for the Coatmen.

From then on, I am told, we kept a watchful eye. More than anyone else, my father saw that we must be ready for danger. He was then the werowance, the commander of our village, of Powhatan, the place at the head of the waterfall. His vision told him what must be done. All the different villages of our people had to band together to be strong for when our enemies returned from the sunrise. My father's vision was strong. Some joined his great alliance willingly. Other villages only gave in after we made war upon them and defeated them. My father became Mamana-towic, Great Chief of all the villages, the Powhatan. All decisions for peace or war were now made through him and his council of advisers. So it was that word was quickly brought to him about the arrival of these new Tassantassuk.

Some prepared to fight, especially the Rappahannocks. Only three winters ago, a swan canoe like these three had come to our shore bearing Outsiders who called themselves Songleesuk. Those Songleesuk visited my father. The Great Man of those Songleesuk, who was very tall, said he came to trade with us and wanted to be our friend. This pleased my father. Perhaps these new Coatmen were different. He gave them permission to trade with our villages. The new Coatmen then took their big ship up the Rappahannock River. The werowance of Rappahannock made them welcome. But the Songleesuk did not continue to behave as guests should. They did something awful.

It is said that the strangers did that awful thing because a Rappahannock man picked up one of their tools as if to carry it away with him. It is hard to believe that. Why would anyone hurt another person for only picking up a tool? But perhaps it is so. One of the strange things about Coatmen is that many of them seem to value their possessions over friendship or human lives. For whatever reason, the tall Great Man of the Tassantassuk pointed his thunder stick and killed the man who had picked up the tool. Then the other Coatmen fired their thunder sticks, too. They killed the werowance of Rappahannock, burned the town, took some of the shocked villagers as captives, and sailed away. So it was that the Rappahannocks swore they would fight the Coatmen if they ever returned.

Many of our own people, though, hoped that these new Coatmen would finally be different. Perhaps they would be true friends. After all, some Tassantassuk had learned to live peacefully among us. Those Outsiders came to the outer shore five returnings of the leaves before I was born. They made a small village on the island Roanoak. Then their swan ship left them. They were abandoned so long by their own countrymen that they began to starve. All would have died without the help of our people. Finally, the surviving Coatmen took off their coats. Outsiders no longer, they joined us. Some of them came to live at Chesepiock. It is sad what happened to Chesepiock because of the prophecy. Because of the prophecy, my father used his power of life to wipe out that village.

As my father's favorite daughter, I sit close to his feet. Others fear him for his power, but I do not. His power, though, is greater than that of any other man. Our many villages trusted

5

my father so much that when they came together under his leadership, they gave him the power of life.

"Why is this so?" I asked my wise older brother, Naukaquawis. "Why does our father have the right to order another person's death?"

"In the days of our father's father," he explained, "whenever there was great wrong done to someone, that man or his relatives would seek revenge and injure or kill the one who had done wrong. Throw, I am ready."

Naukaquawis, who died into manhood six returnings of the leaves ago, knows many things. Although he is no longer a boy and thus does not play with me as he did when he was younger, we still talk together about things. Also, I help him when he practices with his bow and arrow. All of our men are great shots. A boy is given his first bow almost as soon as he can walk. It is the job of his mother to help him practice early every morning by tossing things up into the air for him to shoot at. To make it more interesting, that boy may be denied his morning meal if he misses too many times. Since our mother is no longer with us, I have taken on the task of making sure that Naukaquawis stays sharp as an arrow point now that he is a man. In return, he must always answer anything I ask him. I have at least one question for every arrow he shoots.

"What happened then?" I asked, tossing a ball of moss back and forth between my hands. Then, *"Hi-yah!"* I shouted, as I threw it high up into the air. It had not even reached the height of my throw before Naukaquawis's arrow pierced it.

"Then," Naukaquawis continued, not even bothering to take another arrow from the quiver on his back, "the relatives of that person who had been punished would themselves seek revenge. It went back and forth like this so much that there was always fighting between not only different families but also their villages."

"So what could be done to stop this?" I said. *Yah-hey!* I cried, throwing the second ball of moss as hard as I could over his head and to his left.

With a motion so fast that his hand blurred like a bird's wing, Naukaquawis whipped an arrow from his quiver, nocked it to his bow, spun, and let loose his shot. This time he hit the ball of moss as it was descending.

"When the power to judge and punish wrongdoing was taken out of the hands of individuals and given to our father," he continued, "that fighting ended."

"Why is that so?" I asked. Then I lifted up my hand as if to throw the ball of moss in it. "You will get no breakfast at all if you miss this one," I said. Then I hurled the second moss ball, which I'd concealed in my other hand.

My brother was not fooled. He did not even look toward the target as he let his arrow go. It struck the target and pinned it to the trunk of a mulberry. Then he made a face at me, squinting his eyes and thrusting out his lips.

I made one back, sticking out my tongue, and he laughed. But it did not stop him from giving his answer. "Now we have peace between our villages because all complaints are brought to the Mamanatowic before any fighting takes place. Our father makes his decision, with the quiet counsel of his advisers."

"Like Rawhunt?" I asked.

"Unh-hunh, and others, both women and men. With the help of his council, our father judges who is right or wrong and what punishment must be given."

My brother slung his bow over his shoulder and held out his hand in a gathering motion. We were done with target practice—and questions—for that day. It was now time to retrieve the arrows he had shot.

But he was not done with his words about my father's justice. "Those who do great wrong," Naukaquawis said as he pulled the arrow from the trunk of the mulberry, "such as willfully killing another person, those wrongdoers may even be put to death by our father's orders."

I grew silent at that. I do not like the thought of people being put to death. I do not like the stern, sad look that giving such commands brings to my father's face. But I know how to make him laugh. All I have to do is dance, or stand upon my hands, or sing to him. Then his stern face breaks into a smile. I know how much he appreciates the fact that I can always bring him laughter. He likes to have me by his side.

So I was there on that day in the season before the leaves returned in his great bark-covered longhouse. He waited, sitting in great dignity upon his bench covered with woven mats and padded with leather pillows that were beautifully decorated with shells. I listened with excitement as my father, Powhatan, the Mamanatowic, received the message about the coming of three swan canoes.

My father nodded calmly.

"We will not attack them," he said. "I will keep my eyes upon these Tassantassuk in their swan ships. We do not know yet if they are friends or not, but we are ready. We are ready for peace . . . or war."

2

JOHN SMITH

✦◆✦◆✦◆✦◆✦◆✦◆✦◆✦◆✦◆✦

Aboard

In the year 1606 Captain Newport, with three ships,
discovered the Bay of Chessiopeock in the height of thirty-
seven degrees of northerly latitude, and landed a hundred
persons of sundry qualities and arts in a river falling into it;
and left them under the government of a president and
council, according to the authority derived from and limited
by his Majesty's letters patents.*

—FROM A TRUE & SINCERE DECLARATION
BY THE COUNCIL OF VIRGINIA

DECEMBER 19TH, 1606–MARCH 1ST, 1607

MY NAME, DEAR READER, is John Smith. I am, indeed,
that same Captain John Smith, Gentleman, of whom
others have lately spoken. I take pen to paper to give answer to
certain questions that have arisen about my enterprize in fair
Virginia, how our plantation there did come to be, our relation
with the naturals of that land, the weak judgement in danger
and less in peace of certain of those who were called our leaders,
how I did provide for others neglecting for myself, &tc., &tc.

*By the old reckoning of time, the new year did not begin until the spring. By modern reck-
oning, the arrival date of the English colonists was 1607.

First, one might ask, why did it take so long? It might well be thought a country as fair as Virginia is, and a people so tractable, would long ere this have been quietly possessed to the satisfaction of the adventurers and the eternizing of the memory of those that effected it. But because all the world do see a defailment, this following treatise of mine shall give satisfaction to all readers how the business hath been carried. Then, no doubt, they will easily understand and find answer to their question how it came to pass there was no better speed and success in these proceedings.

❖❖❖❖❖

Captain Bartholomew Gosnoll was one of the first movers of our plantation. For many years he solicited his friends for help, but found small assistance. At last he prevailed with some gentlemen as myself, Master Edward Maria Wingfield, Master Robert Hunt, and diverse others. We then waited a year upon his projects. It was only with our great charge and industry that certain of the nobility, gentry, and merchants spoke in our favor. More than five hundred pounds of my own estate was invested in this pursuit. So at last, on April 10th, 1606, His Majesty King James I affixed his seal to letters patent granting our London Company the right to settle in Virginia.

Now, near another year was spent to effect this. By this time three ships were provided. None of them were over large. The French man-of-war on which I, John Smith, did sail from North Africa to the Canaries (where I engaged in battle two Spanish warships) was twice the size of our flag ship. In point of fact, every one of the ships on which our hopeful company sailed to the new land was smaller, even that ill-favored vessel upon which I once took passage from Marseilles.

Long shall I remember how when a Mediterranean storm

came upon us, the rabble of pilgrims of diverse nations going to Rome cursed both myself and our dread Sovereign Queen Elizabeth. Saying they should never have fair weather as long as I was among them, they then threw me overboard. Yet, God did provide for John Smith. As has so often been the case, foul fortune brought me fair. I swam to a small isle, where I was rescued by the good Captain la Roche of San Malo. Joining his company, we met with an argosy of Venice. When they fired upon us, we gave them back a broadside and bloodily fought until they yielded. As reward for my part in the taking of that ship, I was given five hundred chicqueenes and a little box made of gold worth near as much more and was set well financed down upon the coast of Italy. But, interesting as that tale of my adventure may be and though my readers may surely wish to hear more of my telling of it, there is no time for that now. I must, perforce, return to the matter of Virginia.

Our flag ship was the *Susan Constant*, seventy feet in length, one hundred and twenty tons. Its captain was Christofer Newport. Though he had lost one arm in battle with the Spanish, Captain Newport had crossed the Atlantic several times. The *Godspeed*, forty feet long and forty tons, was captained by Bartholomew Gosnoll himself. The third of our ships, the *Discovery*, was but a pinnace of twenty tons, scarce thirty feet long. Captain John Ratliffe—or so he called himself at that time—held its command.

The names of them that were the first planters are these following:

COUNCEL

Master Edward Maria Wingfield
Captain Bartholomew Gosnoll

Captain John Smith
Captain John Ratliffe
Captain John Martin
Captain George Kendall

GENTLEMEN

Master Robert Hunt, preacher
Master George Percie
Anthony Gosnoll
George Flower
Captain Gabriell Archer
Robert Fenton
Robert Ford
William Bruster
Jehu Robinson
Thomas Wotton, chirugeon
& thirty-nine other gentlemen

CARPENTERS

William Laxon
Edward Pising
Thomas Emry
Robert Small

Anas Todkill
John Capper
James Read, blacksmith
Jonas Profit, sailor
Thomas Cowper, barber
John Herd, bricklayer
William Garret, bricklayer
Edward Brinto, mason

William Love, tailor
Nicholas Scot, drummer
William Wilkinson, chirugeon

LABORERS

John Laydon
William Cassen
George Cassen
Thomas Cassen
William Rodes
& seven others

BOYS

Samuell Collier
Nathaniell Pecock
James Brumfield
Richard Mutton

—with divers others to the number of 105.

On the 19th of December, 1606, we set sail from Black-wall. We had expected the crossing to take but ten weeks. However, from the start, our voyage was not easy. Unprosperous winds kept us long in the sight of England in the Downs off the east coast of Kent. Master Hunt, our preacher, was so weak and sick that few expected his recovery. Yet, though he was but twenty miles from his habitation, he preferred the service of God in so good a voyage. With the water of patience and his godly exhortations, he quenched the flames of envy and dissension. Six full weeks passed before we finally were able to leave the Downs and set out at last across the uncertain ocean.

Even then, all did not go easy for us. The waves were high and most aboard knew little of sailing. Their fears were as great as their stomachs were weak. My oft-told tales of my own adventures, of how I managed to overcome far greater hardships than this voyage, gave comfort to many of our company. When a blazing star did arc above our heads on the night of February twelfth, some among us saw it as an omen of doom. Yet our good captains continued on. At last, nearly ten weeks after setting forth, we had sailed no farther than the Canary Islands. The greater part of our ocean journey still lay before us when, on the first of March, we landed on those islands and took on water.

That half of those among us were gentlemen, and more accustomed to give orders than to engage in work, would cause much sorrow, both on ship and in Virginia. Not only I, but others took note of how the gentlemen would not dirty their hands with work of any sort on ship or land. So it was that I, who did not forswear either labor or the company of our good sailors, came to be in the disfavor of those perfumed dandies who lazed about. It was whilst in the Canaries that an incident occurred and the haughty wrath of certain of those gentlemen was settled upon me.

Vincere est vivere. To conquer is to live. Such has been my motto since I first earned my coat of arms. There were many among our gentlemen planters who un-gently did elevate themselves in my presence. Yet they had no answer when I asked which of them had done battle against the Turk, as did John Smith. There was, indeed, little courage among those who styled themselves my betters.

The most puffed up among them, Edward Maria Wingfield, went so far as to lie that I had begged across Ireland. True it is that I am of good family but not of noble birth. Unlike Wingfield, a man impressed by his own sense of superior birth

and position, I fully earned whatever rank I have held. Edward
Maria Wingfield was born into a knightly family, their seat at
the castle Kimbolton in Huntingdonshire. Yet his father was a
papist and he, himself, has been suspected of Popery. It was
perhaps his wish to appear a good Protestant that led him to
become a soldier by profession. (Though we have also heard it
voiced that he suffered from youthful excesses and premature
debt and escaped both by taking up arms.) He then served in
Ireland and in the Netherlands. Who did he fight there but
other Christians (servants of Rome though they might be)?
And how did Wingfield distinguish himself but by being taken
captive at Lisle in 1588 to be exchanged for Spanish prisoners
taken by Drake?

I, myself, also did battle in the low countries against other
Christians when I was but nineteen. However, I found little joy
in such work. I was both lamenting and repenting to have seen
so many Christians slaughter one another. So when I returned
home, I repaired to a woody pasture. There I made a pavilion of
boughs and lived the life of a hermit with but one man to serve
as my squire. With me I had but two books. The former was
a collection of the sayings of the Roman philosopher and emperor Marcus Aurelius. The latter was Niccolò Machiavelli's
The Art of War.

In that humble field, with my horse and lance, I practiced
the arts and crafts of knighthood. Lord Willoughby, my father's
neighbor and noble friend, was so impressed by my devotion
that he sent to me Master Theodore Paloga, the most famous
horseman in Europe. I grew in skill under Paloga's tutelage until
my horse and I were one creature. I could wield both sword and
lance while riding at full gallop and force my steed to turn on a
shilling. Then, well prepared for battle, I set out again into the
world, vowing to fight only the enemies of Christendom, like

those knights of old who were far nobler than I could ever hope to be. Perhaps, dear reader, I shall later tell more of those adventures. But now I must return to my own restraint.

What then can be said about those circumstances that led to this humble knight's confinement aboard ship during those first days in distant Virginia? Two words alone may suffice. Envy and spite. To explain this I must go back and tell of what befell before we touched on the soil of the new world.

The great strain of our voyage had made tempers short. Immoderate words were oft spoken. As I have earlier told, by the time we fell with the Canaries, we had been at sea a full two and a half months. Through the skillfullness of our Admiral, we had suffered no great loss or danger. Having taken sail many times before, I was not as affected by the sea as were others on board. Some were close to death from seasickness. So, when we came to those whistling islands, I chose to tell yet another of my entertaining stories to take their minds from their troubles.

I modestly told of how in Hungary I, John Smith, engaged, one after the other, three Turkish champions. These were, to wit, the Lord Turbashaw, one Grualgo, and Bonny Mulgro. By the skill of my sword I defeated each and took their heads as trophy. I then related the instructive tale of how, in dismal battle late in 1602, not long after winning my coat of arms, our forces were so overwhelmed that at the end I stood alone among the slaughtered dead bodies of my comrades, who had resolutely ended their days in defense of Christ and his Gospel. Then captured, I was delivered to the young and beauteous Turkish noblewoman Chratza Tragabigzanda, who took much compassion on me.

Even as I related these tales to an appreciative throng of planters and mariners alike, those haughty gentlemen mostly un-gently came upon me.

"Take the traitor," Wingfield snarled.

I forebore from struggle, though my sword was at my side. In truth, I knew I had done no wrong and could not imagine their charges would be believed.

Envying both the admiration of our crew and my repute, Wingfield and his cronies then accused me of diverse crimes. The orders for government had been put in a box not to be opened, nor the governors known, until our arrival in Virginia. The petty plotters feigned that I, John Smith, intended to usurp the government, murder the council, and make myself king. They scandalously suggested that my confederates were dispersed in all the three ships and that diverse of my confederates who had revealed my plot would affirm it. So, though there was never no such matter, I was committed as a prisoner.

The penalty for such mutiny is death. This was the aim of their plan, and failing that, they hoped to make the name of John Smith so odious to the world as to touch his life or utterly overthrow his reputation. The importance and reputation of those gentlemen who sought my ruin was so great that I was restrained from then on. Our good Captain and many others misdoubted those words spoken against me. So, though restrained, I was not kept in irons nor—most fortunately— relieved of my personal arms.

When we fell with the island of Nevis, on the twenty-seventh of March, the eight days that we stayed there gave opportunity for those who hated John Smith to complete their plan. Upon the third day, I was informed, most casually, I would be suffered to go ashore. I was curious to see this island. Indeed, I wondered also what labors had been taking place upon the shore, for the sound of sawing and hammering had drifted over the calm water. Ere I climbed down into the longboat, good John Collson, one of the mariners who had befriended me and harked to my stories, plucked my sleeve.

"Captain," Collson whispered, "I beg ye to be cautelous. I doubt the subtlety of them who doth hate ye."

I feigned not to hear his words, grateful though I was. The warning surprised me not. I had yet made sure that I was well braced and ready. I stood in the front of the longboat and sprang onto the beach before any man could close with me. Seeing their erstwhile victim so ready, no one was ready to see him restrained, least of all those gentlemen who were waiting my arrival by the foot of their construction. Not seeing me before I was upon them, their conversation was how they would now for once and all have done with the odious Smith. They shrank back in shock when I came upon them. The warrior Wingfield was chief of those to lead their hasty retreat.

I walked about their construction, whistling a small merry tune. My hand on the hilt of my cutlass, I gave their work a most careful examination. Well built that structure was, indeed. It was as fine a pair of gallows as might be seen in the Indies. Having satisfied my curiosity, I then did walk up from the beach and hewed a limb from a tree. Thrusting my sword point first in the sand before me, I took out my sharp poignard and carved that branch into a lovely bastinado, a club well suited for the cracking of thick skulls. I waited with great patience, but none approached me.

Alas, though they had labored hard upon that pair of gallows, Captain Smith, for whom they were intended, could not be persuaded to use them.

Thus it was that I spent a pleasant and unmolested several days upon the island of Nevis. When we set sail on April fifth, it was noted that someone had fired that subtle construction. The smoke that rose from the unused gallows was visible for many miles as we continued on our way.

3

POCAHONTAS

❖◆❖◆❖◆❖◆❖◆❖◆❖◆❖

Dressing Myself

The Great Circle of the five good seasons then was made for the people, made by Great Ahone. The first of the seasons is Cattapeuk, when all of the leaves swell again on the trees. The second is sweet Cohattayough, when the berries are ripe and sweet. Nepinough is the season when the corn forms ears. Good Taquitock is the harvest season, when the leaves fall from the trees. Last of all is Cohonk, when the Geese fly in with the coming of the cold. Hardest of all the seasons, still it may seem the shortest of all. For we know well that when it is done, Cattapeuk and the leaves shall return again.

COHATTAYOUGH
TIME OF RIPE BERRIES
EARLY MAY 1607

THE NEW TASSANTASSUK have now made a camp for themselves. They have tied their swan canoes to the big trees along our river and put up small shelters made of white skins that look like the wings of their big boats. The place they have chosen to camp was once also a camping place of our people, close to the village of Paspahegh.

Because of the place they have chosen, it seems that they do not intend to grow crops. The soil is poor on that head of land, too marshy and close to the salt. Also, as my father noted, there seem to be no women among them. Women know the plants and can coax the corn and beans and squash from the soil. Only the tobacco likes best the touch of a man's hands. Since there are no women, my father believes that these men may be here to fight. Men without women are more likely to make war and behave recklessly. Women are always a sign and a means of peace.

Still, I am greatly curious about these Coatmen. I would like very much to visit them. As the daughter of the Great Chief, I can go where I choose, well protected by those who travel with me. And surely even these new Coatmen would not dare to mistreat someone such as myself.

❖·❖·❖·❖·❖

My father has three times seen the death of nearly all his people. It is true that he has watched the leaves return eighty times. Most of those who were young with him have gone to the high place and stepped onto the road to the sunset. But it is not because of his age that this is true. Nor did so many of his people die because of the wars through which he forged our great alliance of seventy tribes. It was the sicknesses. New diseases came among us after the Tassantassuk touched our shore. Those sicknesses burned through our villages like fire through the dry grasses in summer. Some of our people believe that those sicknesses will continue to come as long as the Coatmen keep arriving.

Death does seem to follow the Tassantassuk. Each time the Coatmen arrive, soon after we see new illnesses that our medicines cannot touch. My father says that we must watch the new Coatmen closely and see if they are already sick. Some in the village want to just wipe them out, but my wise father believes we must watch and wait.

I do not doubt that our warriors could defeat the Coatmen, even with their thunder weapons. Our fighters are the strongest and bravest of all men. To make them so strong and brave, we have the ceremony of the *Huskanaw*—which gives one a new body. During that long ordeal, a boy is taken by his keeper into the forest to die and be reborn as a warrior. But even our bravest warriors do not want to kill all our enemies. We know that even the worst enemies may be made into allies. The only nation of which I know that has been wiped from the Great Circle of the earth is that of the Chesepiock, because of the prophecy that a nation would arise from the Chesepiock Bay that would bring an end to my father's great confederacy.

But even then, all the Chesepiocks were not killed when my father made war on them to defeat that prophecy. It was not the people but their nation that was seen by my father as a great threat. After the Chesepiock warriors were defeated, their name as a tribe was extinguished like a burning log dropped into the river. Their women and children were not harmed but adopted among us. Their people were scattered among our other nations and given new names so that the prophecy could not come to pass.

❖❖❖❖❖

This morning, I rose, as I always do, before Kefgawes, the Great Sun, showed itself. I walked down to the river and washed myself in its cold, clean water. I sat by its banks. I made a small circle of tobacco around me. Then I spoke to Kefgawes, giving thanks that I was able to see a new day, that there is strength in my body to move about, that my people and I have been given the things needed to live.

I then went back to my place in my father's house and took out my paint. I chose red paint, made from puccoon, the

21

bloodroot, and the oil crushed from hickory nuts. I stirred it well to make it even and smooth, and I painted my whole face, from the top of my head down to my chin. As is the case for all girls before they reach the age of marriage, my hair is all cut off except for the single long braid at the back of my head. I also painted my shoulders, but I stopped applying paint before reaching the intricate tattoos of intertwined flowers that circle the upper parts of my arms. Those tattoos were made only two seasons ago. I remember the feeling of the sharp bone awl piercing my skin again and again as drops of paint were applied to the places where blood welled up. Of course, I did not cry out or show in any way that I felt the pain. I appreciated the great care that my aunts and my mothers took to make me so beautiful by giving me the tattoos.

As I applied my paint, I used the three long fingers of my right hand and then those of my left. One of my mothers, Green Reed, the oldest of my father's wives, watched as I did all this. She made sure the paint was smooth and even and that I had not missed any places. She painted the white circles around my eyes first and with the fingers of her right hand used more red paint to touch up the places I missed. I had to use the eyes of Green Reed to tell me how I looked.

"Close your eyes," Green Reed said as she dipped her left hand into a box of *matchqueon*, the beautiful dust made by grinding a certain stone. It makes one's face sparkle with many lights that are almost as bright as the twinkling of the Pummahumpal, the distant ones far above, the stars that fill the night sky.

I did as Green Reed said. The warm touch of her breath struck my face as she blew the dust evenly over the still-moist paint. Then I sat without moving until it dried, feeling it tighten the skin of my cheeks as it did so. When it was dry, I stood up and finished dressing myself. The weather has been warm enough to wear no clothing at all—which is the way most of us go about when we are children. However, I was dressing to impress these new Tassantassuk. I would present myself as the favorite daughter of the Great Chief. So I put around my waist a fine white apron of deerskin, which had been softened by tanning with smoke. The apron was decorated with *rawrenock* shells and pieces of copper, making designs in the shapes of animals and flowers. I hung long earrings of strung pearls through the pierced lobes of my ears and then wound a long necklace of pearls and pieces of copper around my neck so that it hung across my bare chest.

Green Reed looked me over and then nodded in approval, as did the other women. I had chosen eight girls of my own age to accompany me. Several of them also were very well dressed, but no one looked as beautiful as I did. They had brought rattles with them, as I had told them to. It was my plan for us to sing a welcoming song and then dance for the Tassantassuk. I could already see in my mind how pleased their strange, hairy faces would be as they saw and heard us emerging from the forest. It would be such fun!

However, as I stood there, the pleased center of attention, someone scratched on the door and then politely cleared his throat.

"*Aho.* You may enter," Green Reed called out.

A head topped by a headdress of hawk feathers and weasel tails appeared under the doorway. The many earrings of copper that dangled from the lobes of both ears clinked together as that person raised his head. The lined and weathered face beneath the headdress was one I knew well. It was Rawhunt. He looked at me, spread his hands, and then brought them down toward the earth. I smiled, even though the paint on my face made it difficult to do so. He was telling me how grateful he was to have been given this glimpse of my beauty. Rawhunt is the perfect emissary. He always knows the right thing to say or do. Although his body has been twisted by his years, he is my father's favorite messenger and a trusted adviser. I was pleased to see him this morning, for it was Rawhunt I wished to accompany me when I visited the new Coatmen. When the Tassantassuk came out to welcome us and praise our singing and dancing and give us presents, Rawhunt could speak for us— and also help carry back whatever gifts we received.

"Amonute," Rawhunt said, speaking my formal name. "Amonute." It was another way of telling me how grand I looked, while also giving me the honor I deserved as my father's daughter.

"Rawhunt," I replied. "It is good to see you are well. I give thanks to Ahone."

"It is good to see that you are well also, good to see," Rawhunt said.

"Are you ready for our journey?" I said.

Rawhunt did not answer quickly. He is careful with his words. He often repeats them, as if enjoying to hear their sound. Much as he likes his own words, though, he likes silence just as well. He began to study the palm of his left hand, as if he had found something interesting there that needed all of his attention. I became suspicious.

"Rawhunt," I said, "what has my father sent you to tell me?"

"*Waugh,*" Rawhunt said. "I am amazed, amazed. How is it that you know your father has sent me to tell you something?"

"Just tell me," I said. I was impatient and not pleased at what I thought I was about to hear.

"Amonute," Rawhunt said, his eyes now on the wall of the lodge, "your father, your father says that perhaps, perhaps this is not the right time for you to visit the Tassantassuk. He has decided that first, first we must see what kind of warriors they are."

4

JOHN SMITH

Ashore

The six and twentieth day of April, about four o'clock in the morning, we descried the land of Virginia; the same day we ent'red into the Bay of Cheupioc directly without any let or hindrance, there we landed and discovered a little way, but we could find nothing worth the speaking of but fair meadows and goodly tall trees, with such fresh waters running through the woods as I was almost ravished at the first sight thereof.

—FROM OBSERVATIONS GATHERED OUT OF
A DISCOURSE OF THE PLANTATION OF THE SOUTHERN COLONY
IN VIRGINIA BY THE ENGLISH, 1606.
WRITTEN BY THAT HONORABLE GENTLEMAN,
MASTER GEORGE PERCY.

APRIL 22ND–APRIL 26TH, 1607

WE PASSED, ON THE twenty-second of April, through a storm so great that it seemed the ocean was one great mouth and all our small fleet would be swallowed up. At last it passed, but it was with tattered sails and great misgiving that we continued on our way, fearing we were lost and our destination would ne'er be reached. Aboard the *Discovery,* Captain Ratliffe urged that our fleet should turn, like whipped curs with our tails between our legs, and flee back toward the safety of England.

"We are near," Captain Newport assured those of faint hearts, yet he knew that we must soon make land or all would be lost indeed. He stood hour after hour on the highstern deck of the *Susan Constant*, eyes squinted against the glare of sun and sea, seeking the welcome sight of land as others sank further into despair.

Yet, as so often happens, fair did follow foul. Ere the full light of dawn, at four o'clock in the morning, came the cry.

"Land ho!"

There rose the southernmost point of land that guards the entry to Chesapeake. The sun lifting from the wide sea behind us shone its light on that very bay which had been our destination. God, the guider of all good actions, had driven us by His providence to our desired port beyond all our expectations. As we watched, a great-winged bird lifted from the marshy land and flapped its way across the sky, passing slowly over the bow of our flag ship.

Our little armada made its way, led by our admiral, through shoals and bars to anchor at last in a likely place not far from shore. The place that lay before us seemed goodly, indeed. To the eyes of men who had seen too much of wave after wave, the green trees and the pleasant meadows were almost as welcome as the sight of home and family left behind. Before them lay a fruitful and delightsome land. Their eagerness to set foot on this new shore was, sad to say, as great as their heedlessness. No real soldier was among the party that left the safety of our ships.

Some thirty men, led by Captain Newport, himself, took to the boats. Soon they had left their footsteps behind them in the sand as they climbed up from the beach to look upon the new land. 'Twas not an easy climb, for the ground was marshy, tangled with reeds and other strange grasses. Before them, on the higher land, grew goodly taller trees, oak, walnut, and pine, next to fair meadows where fresh waters ran through the woods. The day was warm, and I know well how hot and heavy their armor and breastplates must have felt to them. Yet a man used to war also grows used to such discomforts, which are far less than the pain of an arrow piercing unguarded flesh. Had I been among that less than cautelous party, I would have warned them to keep closer guard and never doff their helms.

But where was this wise Captain Smith on that first day when our party began discovering this new land? Where was he while the naturals did peer from hiding and then creep silent as bears, their bows held in their teeth, closer and closer to that heedless band of gentlemanly innocents? Why did he not urge them to find a place easier to defend? As the one true soldier among them, why did he not make them set proper sentries and urge them to keep their eyes open for fear of subtlety from the naturals?

Alas, I, John Smith, was still held on board our Admiral, the *Susan Constant,* laid by the heels as a prisoner. Whereas I had spurned the invitation to my own execution, I remained still in ill favor among those favored notables on board when we reached the new land. I could but watch, pacing back and forth on the deck of our flag ship, as the landing party went ashore.

The day passed without incident. From time to time one of our party, perhaps the eager Percy or the portly Wingfield, would appear on the crest of a hill to wave in joy or derision at those of us left behind on board.

"All is well," would drift the call across the still water.

Then that unrestrained adventurer would vanish again from sight to delight in the feel of land beneath his feet, the scent of pines, or the wild red berries which grew in abundance and were most sweet to the taste.

At last, as the light began to fail and the soft breeze of evening to blow, our landing party made ready for their return to our ships. I watched as best I could, apprehensive, for I know how perilous is that hour when the coming night cloaks danger in its growing shadows. A true warrior may oft find ways to turn the dark to his advantage. Indeed, that coming night reminded me of one of my own adventures.

It happened whilst in Hungary, where I had joined the army of Baron Hans Jacob Kisell, who was seeking to relieve the Christians of Oberlimback who were beseiged by the Turks. Having studied my military texts so well, I was able to suggest to him a way of using our torches as signals in battle. In the dark, our pagan enemy estimated our numbers by counting the number of fuses burning atop our pieces. My conclusion was that two or three thousand pieces of match fastened to diverse small lines of a hundred fathom in length and attached to two staves might all be fired at once. Being discovered by those false fires, the Turks would think them to be some great army. So it did happen. As the Turks made ready to face our false army, Kisell and his ten thousand attacked the Turks' quarter from behind. A third part of the Turks were slain and all who survived fled. As the author of this plan, I was occasioned a good reward and preferment and made captain of two hundred and fifty horsemen.

That pleasant memory brought a smile to my lips, but my ears were still pricked toward the darkening beach. Just as I feared, before our unwise adventurers could reach their boat, their alarums sounded from shore.

"Take arms, take arms," came the desperate shout across the wine-dark water. "The salvages are upon us."

Then followed the war cries and the sound of fighting. I saw the flashes of fire from our pieces, heard the shouts of confusion and pain which always accompany a battle. Though I did not know it then, Captain Gabriell Archer was wounded in both hands, and one of the sailors was pierced by arrows two places in his body very grievously. Indeed, with no man among our party on shore who knew anything of warfare, our whole enterprize might have ended there had the naturals fallen upon them in great numbers.

Some few among us had the sense to fire upon them from the pinnace, which was close enough to shore. They felt the sharpness of our shot. Howbeit, 'twas only after that party of salvages, which was blessedly small and poorly armed, had spent all their arrows that they retired into the woods with a great noise and left us.

I could but clench my fist and pound it upon the rail as I stared into the dark Virginia night. Yet even as I harked to the attack of the naturals and heard the wails of our wounded, the thought went through my mind that my restraint would soon be at an end. Having felt the sharpness of arrows, the planters would now feel differently. The need of a soldier's knowledge would be seen with the light of day.

5

POCAHONTAS

Enemies or Friends

We make offerings to those powers that help us. We give tobacco to the medicine plants, to the earth from which springs the corn. We sing and speak out thanks to Okeus and the many kwiokosuk who help us see what approaches through the eyes of their priests.

We keep thanks in our hearts, for we know that Great Hare has a lodge prepared for us beyond the rising Sun. When a spirit is ready to leave this earth, it first goes treetop-high. There it sees a broad, flat path that is easy to travel. That path leads toward the sunrise. Along its sides grow ripe berries and fruits of all kinds. Halfway on the journey, the spirit rests for a while in the lodge of the Good Woman Spirit. There it is given hominy and hickory-nut milk. At the end of that road to the rising Sun, the spirit of one who has died comes to Great Hare's lodge. There those who have gone before greet that spirit with delight. They dance and sing with Great Hare and eat good foods of all kinds.

However, the spirits of those who have died from the earth do not stay forever in Great Hare's lodge. They age, though much more slowly than here within this life. At last, when they have grown old and gray, they die and are reborn again as a child into our world.

I DO NOT UNDERSTAND," I said to my father as he sat on his mat, restringing a necklace of pearls. Although he is Mamanatowic and might ask others to do such things for him, my father still prefers to do as all the other men do. He makes his own mockasins, works with his own hands the copper that he shapes into earrings or ornaments for his hair, and sews together his own fine robes from Arakun skins. "If the Coatmen are such enemies that I cannot visit them, why do we not just drive them away?"

"Matoaka," he said in a soft voice. I drew closer to him. My father had called me by the name that only my closest family knows. It means Snow Floating Down Like Feathers. Clearly he wished his words to go to my heart.

"I am listening," I said, resting my hands on his knees.

My father laid the necklace of pearls across his lap and placed his hands on my shoulders. "*Nechaun,* my child, I see that these new Tassantassuk are not like the Espaniuk. Maybe they will be of use to us. They have strong weapons. Maybe I will be able to use them and their weapons against our enemies."

My father's words were wise. Still, for it is my nature, I had to ask him another question.

"If they will be our friends, why do you not send for them? Bring them here to Werowocomoco to see how great you are and swear allegiance to you."

My father smiled at my words. "Favorite daughter," he said, "I may do just that. But first we must be patient. I have sent word to our villages that each may do as they wish for now with the Tassantassuk. If they want to fight with them, let them try to do so. If they want to try to be friends with them, that, too, will be their decision."

"Can we not tell all our villages to be friendly to the Coatmen?" I asked.

My father shook his head. "You know how our villages are. If not for my alliance, they would still be fighting each other to no good purpose. So I allow them to each try their own way. For now. And I will watch. This way I will see what sort of people these Coatmen are."

With that he removed his hands from my shoulders and took up his string of pearls again.

❖◆❖◆❖

I have done as my father asked and not gone to the camp of the Coatmen. Of course, I do not always do what he tells me. I come and go as I choose and do what I want to do. Sometimes, I am told I get in the way of others when I do this. But I have found that if I make a joke of it, if I make faces or go tumbling head over heels, I can make people laugh.

I am sure that with my teasing and my tricks I could make even some of the Coatmen laugh. But probably not all of them. I am told that the Coatmen have such stiff faces that they do not crack easily into a laugh.

Many stories have been coming upriver to us about the Coatmen. Some of them are very hard for me to believe, as hard to believe as the contradictory words the Coatmen speak to our people. First these Tassantassuk say that they are only making a visit to trade. Yet they are now building a strong fort. Then they say that they wish to be friends. Yet they become angry and violent about small things. If any one of our people even touches one of their fire sticks, they beat that person or try to kill him. They beg us to get food for them. But they are just

32

6

JOHN SMITH

The Boxes

That night was the box opened and the orders read in which Bartholomew Gosnoll, John Smith, Edward Wingfield, Christopher Newport, John Ratliffe, John Martin, and George Kendall were named to be the council; and to choose a president amongst them for a year who with the council should govern. Matters of moment were to be examined by a jury but determined by the major part of the council in which the president had two votes.

—FROM THE GENERALL HISTORIE
BY JOHN SMITH

APRIL 26TH–MAY 13TH, 1607

THE GATHERING AND OPENING of the three boxes, one of which had been bestowed in each of our vessels for the trip, was done with great excitement. Too many were interested for it to be done in private, and so much of our company was gathered upon the deck of our Admiral. Despite his hurts, Captain Archer, his hands bound to staunch the blood, did attend. Howbeit restrained, I was allowed to be present. There, no doubt, I would hear the name of my betters spoken and be pressed down yet further into my place of inferiority.

Puffed as a pigeon, the great Edward Maria Wingfield gazed down his nose with a look of perfect superiority before turning his back upon me. Then, with a smile, Wingfield flourished the list as yet unfolded.

"Hear now," he said, "the name of those worthies who shall lead our happy company."

"Edward Maria Wingfield," he intoned, then with false modesty smirked. "Ah, but am I worthy?" He then looked about, more puffed than before, mayhap feeling the mantle of president falling already upon his shoulders.

He cleared his throat and continued, a slow reader, taking but one word at a time, as if picking bits of meat from a platter. "Captain Christopher Newport. Yes, our own good admiral. Bartholomew Gosnoll, a fine gentleman planter. Captain John Ratliffe, ah, what wisdom do our sponsors show."

Then, for he had read ahead a bit on his list, the air went out of the pigeon's chest and his shoulders slumped. He coughed and sputtered as if a fit had come upon him. His countenance darkened. Yet Wingfield could not pause forever, nor could he feign not to read the seventh and final name of those good gentlemen chosen by the Virginia Company. Others, myself amongst them, were already reading the list over the popinjay's rounded shoulder.

"I do misdoubt," Wingfield said in a near whisper that only those closest to him could hear.

"Read on," a rough voice shouted from back in the crowd. It was the seaman John Collson.

Wingfield looked up, a protest near to birthing on his lips. But other voices echoed that call.

"An error," Wingfield said, his voice a bit stronger. "The other copies of the list may correct this."

In fine, the other two boxes divulged their contents. The

lists were seen identical, the reading completed with the speaking of the final two names in that list of seven chosen and most worthy gentlemen.

"George Kendall," Wingfield read. And then, spitting out the words as if bitter medicine, "John Smith."

It was to me no measure of surprise that though chosen I was yet not suffered to serve. An oration was made why Captain Smith was not to be admitted of the council as the rest. Agreement was forged among those special six, the council sworn in, and Master Wingfield was chosen president.

On the seven and twentieth day, we began to build up our shallop that had been brought in pieces from England. A party of gentlemen and soldiers marched eight miles into the land without seeing a salvage in all that march. They did come to a place where a great fire had been made and oysters that had been newly a-roasting were left in the fire. Those oysters, George Percy assured me, were very large and delicate in taste.

On the eight and twentieth day the shallop was launched. The captain and some gentlemen went in her and discovered up the bay. Upon the thirtieth they coasted to a town. The captain called to the naturals in sign of friendship and lay his hand upon his heart. Upon that, the salvages lay down their bows and arrows and welcomed the adventurers to their town of Kecoughtan. Further discovery was made up the river, which has a strong flow and might turn to be that northwest passage that would lead us across the narrow continent to the western ocean.

At length, upon the thirteenth day of May, a place to plant in was chosen next to the river. Linked to the mainland by a narrow neck of land that was quite underwater when the tide was high, it seemed it might be easily defended. Three miles long and a mile in width, it was believed by those who chose it to be a goodly place.

More of that shall be said anon, but none of these discoveries or decisions did include me. I was not yet allowed ashore. Though less ill-favored, I remained quite out of favor.

Now falleth every man to work, though many chose but to work their jaws in telling others what to do. The wise council contrive the fort. Alas, for that. The rest, myself included, cut down trees to make place to pitch their tents, some provide clapboard to relade the ships, some make gardens, some nets, &tc., &tc.

The salvages often visited us kindly, though I did misdoubt that they would always show but the hand of friendship. Our sponsors had urged us to treat the naturals well, but it seemed to me that good treatment doth not rule out wise defense. However, each word I spoke in favor of firm fortifications fell upon unhearing ears.

Our plantation we named James Fort. Yet the president's overweening jealousy would admit no exercise at arms or fortification but the boughs of trees cast together in the form of a half-moon by the extraordinary pain and diligence of Captain Kendall.

7

POCAHONTAS

❖❖❖❖❖❖❖❖❖❖❖❖❖❖❖❖❖❖❖❖

Backwards People

*Long ago, after Ahone made the Sun and Moon and Stars, it
was then that Okeus shaped the earth and all the things upon
it. It is said that Okeus gave us the many kinds of corn and
taught us how to plant them and care for them in the right
way. If we care for these great gifts and give them our love,
they will, in return, give us our lives. We must share these gifts
with all our people and with any who come to us as guests. But
if we do not do as Okeus taught us, great sorrow will surely
come on us and we will be punished.*

NEPINOUGH
TIME WHEN CORN FORMS EARS
LATE MAY 1607

IN THE TWO MOONS that have passed since the new Tassantassuk first arrived, they have done so many strange things.
I find it hard to believe that people could behave as strangely as
they do. It is confusing to me. Though I still wish to see them
and have promised myself that I shall do so, I have decided to
heed my father's advice and wait. Rawhunt tells me each day of
some new and unusual thing done by the newcomers.

They have begun to travel out from their camp, as far up the
river as our village of Powhatan, where my older half brother

Parahunt is werowance. Although they are hungry people, they do not seem to know much about getting food. They are now trying to grow crops in the poor soil of their camping place. There is too much salt from the river there, and the earth they have chosen for planting will be too dry by the time of the summer season. Groups of men from the various villages near them have visited, bringing them gifts of food. But the Coatmen do not always respond in a friendly way, even to gifts. This is especially hard for me to understand. When I am given presents, even small ones, it makes me feel warm and happy in my heart, and I want nothing more than to be kind to those who have gifted me.

The Coatmen seem to like to travel far and wide. That, at least, I can understand. They are as curious as Arakun, wanting to see and touch everything. They have a canoe that is much smaller than the big swan boats. They make it go faster than our bigger dugouts, but they paddle it in a strange way, with their backs turned toward the direction they wish to go. Rawhunt laughed today when he told me of this.

"Perhaps," he said, "these Tassantassuk do everything backwards, everything backwards. For example, I have seen that when it is hot, instead of taking off clothing, they put more on, put more on. And when they are dirty, instead of bathing, they stay away from the water." Then he made such outrageous suggestions about backward things that they might do that I laughed even harder than Rawhunt.

Rawhunt also told me about a strange thing our people have seen the Coatmen do several times. When the Coatmen reach a place they have not been before and they come onshore, they sometimes bring with them a thing made of two posts fastened together, making a shape like that of our design for the four directions. They bury its base in the ground, speak loud words, and then leave it there. Rawhunt thinks it may have something to do with their way of worship.

"Perhaps," Rawhunt said, "perhaps, perhaps, the gods they worship are the four winds, the four winds. Those crosses they bury in the earth may stand for the four directions where the wind spirits live."

When those Tassantassuk first began to travel, a small party of them went to Paspahegh. Wowinchopunck, the werowance of Paspahegh, welcomed them. The newcomers were treated as all guests should be treated. Wowinchopunck's warriors laid their weapons upon the ground. They held out their right hands to link their index fingers with those of the Coatmen. The Coatmen were given much food and good drink. People sang to them and danced. That time, I was pleased to hear, all went well and the Coatmen behaved like proper guests.

A few days later, before they had found the camping spot where they have set up their white lodges, they were given a test when they came to the mouth of the Appamattuck and went ashore. A group of our men met them. Our men were well armed with bows and arrows, monacocks and tomahaks, and each carried a shield made of thick bark that could stop an arrow. But our men were worried. They had been told about the Coatmen's thunder sticks. Still, our men showed no fear. They stood tall as the Coatmen approached. Then the leader of our men put down his shield and stepped forward. He held out both of his hands. In his left hand he held a bow. In his right hand he held a pipe filled with tobacco. Without hesitation, the leader of the Coatmen stepped forward and accepted the tobacco pipe. The choice of war or friendship had been offered, and the Coatmen had taken the pipe of peace.

With great relief, our men sat down with the Coatmen and smoked the pipe together. Our men admired the bright knives and glittering tomahaks of the Coatmen. They liked the way those weapons shone like the sun striking water. It would be good to trade for such fine tools. Our men gave the newcomers food and tried to teach them more of our words, of which they already seemed to know a few, though they spoke them poorly.

"*Wingapo*," the English leader said, tapping himself on the chest to indicate that his heart was good, that he was indeed a "good man" as he had said.

However—and this made me sad when I heard it—just when the people of Paspahegh thought they knew the hearts of these newcomers, the Coatmen again behaved badly. They made their camp without asking the permission of Wowinchopunck or the people of Paspahegh. They began to guard it in a way that did not seem friendly. The people of Paspahegh became worried. Were the Coatmen enemies or friends? Wowinchopunck urged his people to be patient. He decided to go see them and learn if they knew how to treat a guest in the right way. He sent two messengers, painted and dressed in a very fine way, to let the Coatmen know that he would make a visit.

Then, having given the newcomers time to prepare for the visit of a chief, Wowinchopunck went to their camp. He took with him a hundred men and the gift of a fine, big deer. But the Coatmen did not lay down their weapons as had the warriors of Paspahegh. They seemed suspicious and angry. They stared at our men and muttered things to one another. The Paspahegh men held out their hands in friendship, but the Coatmen did not take their hands. Then one of Wowinchopunck's men picked up a Coatman's glittering tomahak.

"*Wingapo*," Wowinchopunck's man said. "Good man."

But the Coatman who kept that tomahak did not behave in a friendly way. He grabbed the tomahak by its handle and twisted it out of the man's grasp. Then he struck the surprised

Paspahegh man hard on the arm with the flat side of the tomahak, bruising him badly. It was a great insult. Some of our people became quite upset.

However, even though they were the ones who had behaved so badly, the Tassantassuk now began to act angry. They shouted loud words to one another. They raised their thunder sticks and pointed them at our people.

Wowinchopunck was deeply offended.

"Pick up the deer," he said. "These rude people do not know how to treat a guest properly."

Then he and all his men turned and walked back across the narrow neck of land. They did not run, but as they left they worried that they would hear the thunder of the unpredictable Coatmen's weapons at their backs.

8

JOHN SMITH

The River

*The river which we have discovered is one of the famousest
that was ever found by any Christian. It ebbs and flows a
hundred and threescore miles where ships of great burthen
may harbor in safety.*

*Wheresoever we landed upon this river we saw the
goodliest woods, as beech, oak, cedar, cypress, walnuts,
sassafrass, and vines in great abundance which hang in
great clusters on many trees, and other trees unknown,
and all the grounds bespread with many sweet and
delicate flowers, mulberries, raspberries, and fruits
unknown.*

*There are many branches of this river which run
flowing through the woods with great plenty of fish of all
kinds; as for sturgeon, all the world cannot be compared to
it. In this country I have seen many great and large
meadows having excellent good pasture for any cattle. There
is also great store of deer, both red and fallow, there are
bears, foxes, otters, beavers, musk cats and wild beasts
unknown.*

*The four and twentieth day, we set up a cross at the
head of this river, naming it "Kings River," where we*

proclaimed James, King of England, to have the most right
unto it.

—FROM OBSERVATIONS GATHERED OUT OF
A DISCOURSE OF THE PLANTATION OF THE SOUTHERN COLONY
IN VIRGINIA BY THE ENGLISH, 1606.
WRITTEN BY THAT HONORABLE GENTLEMAN,
MASTER GEORGE PERCY.

MAY 18TH–27TH, 1607

OUR FIRST ENCOUNTERS with the naturals were such that a wiser man than our president would have had much doubt. The gentleman still refused to impale our small plantation. It remained contrived without wall or strong defense. I urged often that our men be armed and exercised, but my words and myself were scorned. It was still the plan of the wise Wingfield to have Captain Smith referred to the council in England to receive a check for his supposed mutiny. Though restrained, I cautioned the more careful amongst us to keep watchful eyes.

It was well I did so. The eighteenth day of May, the werowance of Paspihae came himself to our quarter. Most of the naturals do go about naked, with only their privities covered by beasts' skins, but it is not so for their kings. Paspihae had dressed himself in his finest, wearing a great robe woven with long feathers and the skin about his waist beset with the teeth of beasts to make designs in the shapes of various creatures. Chains of pearls and shells were about his neck, and more strings of pearls hung from his ears. His body was painted crimson and besprinkled, it seemed, with silver ore. His face was painted watchet, as blue as the sky itself. His hair was tied in a great knot atop his head, and four tall feathers thrust up from his crown of deer's hair dyed red. With him were a hundred more salvages, armed in a most warlike manner and thinking at that time to execute their villainy. They carried bows and arrows, and the swords on their backs were beset with sharp stones and pieces of iron able to cleave a man in sunder.

Paspihae made signs that we should lay down our arms.

I looked to George Percy and the brave gentleman nodded back at me.

"We will not trust him so far," Percy said, holding his piece more firmly.

Our President, though, urged the naturals to join us. Soon they had pushed into the fort and were milling about us in a great throng. Then one bold salvage stole a hatchet from Master Eustace Clovell. Master Clovell spied him doing the deed, whereupon he took the hatchet from him with great force, and also struck him upon the arm. Seeing that, another salvage came fiercely at our man with a wooden sword, thinking to beat out his brains.

"Hold!" Percy cried. Holding his piece at chest height, he stepped in and shoved it against the natural who bore the sword. Off balance, the man stumbled back, his attack forestalled, though a growl arose from among the ranks of the naturals. With that we all took to our arms.

The salvages, who had surely been about to fall upon us, paused. It was well that they did. Our matches were lit, our pieces pointed at their breasts. Paspihae, himself, glared at me and I back at him.

Seeing we could not be taken by surprise, the naturals fell back. And so Paspihae went suddenly away with his company in great anger.

From then on, I was no longer so restrained in my movements. The presence of a man who knew the arts of war was seen at last to be of service. Captain Newport liked me well and joined me to his company that would next adventure up the Kings River. On Thursday, the first and twentieth of May, having fitted our shallop with provisions and all necessities belonging to a discovery, we set out. Our Captain proceeded with a perfect resolution not to return before finding either the head of this river, the sea again, or some issue. The names of the two and twenty discoverers are these:

CAPTAIN CHRISTOFER NEWPORT

GENTLEMEN

Captain John Smith
Captain Gabriell Archer
George Percy, Esquire
Master John Brookes
Master Thomas Wotton

MARINERS

Francys Nelson
John Collson
Robert Tyndall
Mathew Fytch

SAILORS

Jonas Poole
Robert Markham
John Crookdeck
Olyver Browne
Benjamyn White

Rychard Genoway
Thomas Turnbrydg
Thomas Godword
Robert Jackson
Charles Clarke
Stephen
Thomas Skynner

From James Fort we took our leave at noon. By night we were up the river eighteen miles at a low meadow point. The naturals of this place name their kingdom Wynauk. We hailed these Wynauks with words of kindness.

"*Wingapo*," Captain Newport called to them.

"*Wingapo chemuze*," the Wynauks replied, greeting us with much rejoicing. There the people of the kingdom of Wynauk entertained us with dances. The King of Wynauk is at odds with the King of Paspihae and for that we anchored peacefully all night.

By diverse small habitations we passed as we continued up-river. The king of another village, Aratahec, gave us a guide who was Aratahec's brother-in-law. This salvage, Nauiraus, proved to be a trusty friend. In six days, we arrived at a town called Powhatan, some twelve houses pleasantly seated on a hill. Before it are three fertile isles, about it many of their corn-fields, a place pleasant and strong by nature. The prince of this place is called Tanxpowhatan and his people Powhatans. No further might we proceed because of the rocks and isle; there is not passage for a small boat.

Upon one of the little islets at the mouth of the falls, Captain Newport set up a cross. It bore the inscription *Jacobus Rex. 1607* and Newport's own name below. At the erecting we prayed for our king and our own prosperous success. Then, with a great shout, we proclaimed our great James the true king of all this land.

Nauiraus began to admire the meaning of our setting up the cross with such a shout. Our captain calmed his suspicion, telling him that the two arms of the cross signified King Tanx-powhatan and himself. The fastening of it in the middle stood for their united league, and the shout was our reverence we did to Powhatan. This cheered our gullible guide not a little.

During our return, the people in all parts kindly entreated us till we were within twenty miles of James Town. Then our guide, Nauiraus, took some conceit.

"I can go no further with you," he said, his voice most agitated. "I will see you again in three days."

When we placed him upon the shore, he ran so swiftly into the forest that our captain became worried. We made all haste home, fearing some disastrous hap at the fort. It fell out as expected. God had not blessed those at the fort as well as He had blessed the discoverers.

Seeing our absence, the salvages saw a sure opportunity to carry the fort. Upon the fifth and twentieth day of May, above two hundred of them came with their king and gave a furious assault. No sentries had been set. Our men were at work and not ready, their arms in dryfats. The spring grasses had also grown so tall all around our fort that the naturals were able to creep so close that our men were well within the range of their bows when the salvages at last burst from cover with a shout.

"Their cry," Jehu Robinson said to me as he reported the events of that fight, "was so terrible that I near fell down in fright."

Much of the fighting that followed then was hand-to-hand, for our company's lack of ready arms.

"Grim work 'twas indeed," Robinson said, "made e'en worse

by them cries of battle from the salvages that ne'er did cease as they thrust for'ard with fierce intent."

The salvages, a very valiant people, came up almost into the fort, and shot through the tents in this skirmish which endured hot about an hour. Diverse of them were surely killed, but they tugged off the dead on their backs.

Seeing what was happening, the cannoneers aboard the *Susan Constant* aimed their guns at the mass of salvages seeking to thrust their way into our fort. Though the ships' ordnance with their small shot daunted them, they might yet have overthrown our defenders, for each salvage that fell was replaced by two more eager to join the battle.

At last, upon the ship, someone among the cannoneers bethought him to load bar shot, two halves of a cannon ball joined together by a long iron spike. That crossbar, fired into the trees above the heads of the naturals, struck down a great bough among them and caused them to retire.

We found seventeen injured and a boy slain by the salvages. Four of the council that had stood in front were hurt in maintaining the fort. Our president, Master Wingfield, spoke loudly.

"I have shown myself valiant," he said, "valiant indeed."

Indeed, he said this so often to whomever harked that he seemed, at the least, to convince himself. Our brave president had one shot clean through his beard, yet 'scaped hurt. Perhaps this is of no surprise, for Jehu Robinson also noted to me how well Master Wingfield succeeded in always placing himself as far to the back as possible throughout the fray.

Hereupon, I must note, the president was contented that the fort should be pallisadoed, the ordnance mounted, his men armed and exercised.

9

POCAHONTAS

◆◇◆◇◆◇◆◇◆◇◆◇◆◇◆◇◆◇◆◇◆

Many Questions

Great Hare lives in his home in the sunrise. There he made the first women and men. He kept them at first in a great bag. It was well that he did so, for the Four Wind Giants smelled those first women and men and came howling to the lodge of Great Hare. The Wind Giants were then much as they are now, without shape or form, but with the power to knock down great trees and fly through the air with a sound so great that it is frightening.

In they came, howling from each of the directions, from the Winter Land, the Sunrise Land, the Land of Summer, and the Dark Land.

"We are hungry," the Four Wind Giants howled. "Open your bag. Give us those new ones you have made. Open your bag so we can get at them. We will eat them."

Great Hare, though, was not frightened. "No," he said. "Go away."

And the Four Wind Giants did just that.

EVEN THOUGH I HAVE reason to ask more questions than usual today, I am one who always asks many questions. I have heard this said by my father, by Rawhunt, by all of my mothers at one time or another. They do not criticize me when they say this. They just make mention of it in the way one might notice that water is wet.

For example, while other children just listened this past winter while Uttomatomakkin told the story of how we were made, as soon as the old priest stopped to take a breath, I was the one who had to say:

"Why was it that Great Hare made us and not Ahone?"

"It is the way it is," Uttomatomakkin said to me. His voice was patient as he stroked the hairs on his chin with his left hand. Among our people, only the priests allow hair to remain on their faces. All other men pull those hairs out with clamshell tweezers. Uttomatomakkin seems rather proud of those hairs on his chin.

He is the head of all the priests and is so much a favorite of my father's that he is married to one of my father's sisters. Whenever my father has a serious question about the future, he turns to Uttomatomakkin, who then goes into the sacred *yiha-can*, the god's house, and speaks to Okeus. Within the circle of cornmeal, he lays out kernels of corn in lines and counts them. Then he is able to see what things are going to happen. But even a priest, Uttomatomakkin has told me, does not always understand what he sees. Many things, he says, are beyond the understanding of humans. So I was not surprised when he answered my question the way he did. Just like a priest!

"Ah," I said, as if I was satisfied. "But I have another question."

"Of course. I know you will ask it." He stroked his chin hairs again as he looked down at me.

I squinted up at him. Was he making fun of me? There was no trace of a smile on his face, which was still as smooth as a child's, even though he has seen more than eighty returnings of the leaves.

"Who did Great Hare make first? Was it a man or a woman?"

"Why do you ask, Amonute?" Uttomatomakkin replied.

For a priest, answering a question with another question is a common way to respond. Then Uttomatomakkin did smile.

I have always known that he finds me amusing. I do not mind. He is an uncle to me and even funnier than Rawhunt when he wishes to be. Others fear him because he is so close to Okeus, but I do not.

"I ask because it seems to me that it would first have been a woman. After all, it is women who give birth to men and not the other way around."

"Then it may have been that way," Uttomatomakkin said, raising both hands and lifting them toward the sky.

Again, it was a typical answer for a *quiyoughsokuk* to make. The priests do not like anyone to know more than they do about such things as medicine or the power of the spirits. If I were not who I am, the favorite daughter of Powhatan, Uttomatomakkin would not say that much to me. But, then again, who else would ask the sorts of questions that I ask? Like the meaning of my name, questions follow me wherever I go.

Today it was a very sad day. As I walked around the village, I kept thinking of the story of Great Hare and how he protected the first people. I could hear women mourning for a loved one who had been killed by the thunder sticks. Nearby, in the forest, other members of the family of the man who had died were building a burial scaffold on which the body of the departing one would be placed.

Two days ago men from five different villages decided to make an attack on the Tassantassuk. The Coatmen had been wandering around like foolish children shoving sticks at the nests of hornets. They had been going where they should not go, paddling their backward canoe up and down our river, putting up their strange crosses, and confusing people with their actions by promising friendship and then making the same pledge to the enemies of those they had sworn they befriended. They also were insulting to the leaders of our villages, treating them like fools or children.

Opposunoquonuske is the weroansqua of the Appamattuck. Her brother is the werowance, but her voice in council is stronger than his. She is a beautiful woman, as big as a bear, strong and brave. The Coatmen were wise enough to give her gifts, but she did not like their manner. When they fired off their thunder sticks to impress her people, the Coatmen seemed disappointed that she showed no fear. Opposunoquonuske was offended by the smell of the Tassantassuk.

"Standing close to them," she said, "is like being downwind from one of the black-and-white–striped ones."

She would not allow them to sit near her.

When I first heard this, I found it hard to believe that men could smell that badly.

"Do they not bathe every day as we do?" I asked Rawhunt.

Rawhunt shook his head. "Amonute," he said, "listen, listen. In this way, at least, these new Tassantassuk are like the Espaniuk. They seem to fear, yes, fear the touch of water on their bodies. They never wash themselves or remove their heavy coats." Rawhunt laughed. "Perhaps, perhaps it is because they have such love for all the little crawling things that live in the fur on their faces and on their bodies. They do not want to disturb their tiny chums by bathing. I see you shake your head, but what I say is true. It is true. I met some of them when I was younger. Long ago, long ago as it was, I still remember how badly they smelled. Indeed, if you are downwind, it is always easy to tell when a Tassantassa is coming your way. *Waugh,* you can smell him long before you can see him. Long before you can see him. Long before."

Opechancanough, who is my father's younger brother, has also had dealings with Tassantassuk. One of his closest friends was killed by a party of Coatmen led by a very tall man. Another of his friends was wounded by the small stones thrown by a thunder stick and now walks with a limp.

"Those Coatmen," Opechancanough said, "attacked them for no reason." He mistrusts all of these newcomers.

"Hunh," he said to me when I asked if it was true that Coatmen had an unpleasant odor. "Hear what I tell you, my niece. They are foul-smelling ones, it is true. But the things they do are worse than their smell. We should drive all of them away from our lands and waters."

❖❖❖❖

In fact, it was my uncle, Opechancanough, who told me how the attack on the Tassantassuk came about. In only a few handfuls of days the Coatmen had upset and insulted many people. They had angered so many people that villages that had been fighting one another for a generation decided to join together in the attack. Men from the Chiskiacks, the Appamattucks, the Paspaheghs, the Quiyoughcahannocks, and the Wyanocks all took part. They thought that their attack would succeed quickly. They believed that they would kill a few of the Coatmen and discourage the rest so much that they would get into their big swan canoes and go away. They chose a time when the Coatmen who seemed to be the best fighters were away from their camp.

The Tassantassuk turned out to be better fighters than our men had expected. A few of the Coatmen tried to hide, especially one fat Coatman whose beard was so large that an arrow stuck in it. But others stood and faced our warriors bravely. Even when they were wounded, they kept fighting. Their thunder sticks were bad, but our men learned that they could drop to the ground and avoid being hit, as one does when an arrow is fired. Our men were close to victory when the swan boats themselves roared thunder, and our fighters had to retreat. Even though they were beaten, they did not run. They sang and shouted defiance as they backed away. They carried with them all those who had been struck by the Coatmen's weapons.

Twelve men were badly injured. Seven others were killed. One of them, though he had recently gone to live among his friends at Appamattuck, came from our great town. His mother and sisters are still here. His body had been brought to them at dawn by his companions. It was the voices of those who loved him that I heard weeping and crying. Their faces blackened the dark color of grief, they wailed for the loss of their beloved one.

Wearing his finest jewelry, necklaces, and earrings of shells and copper, wrapped in deerskins, he would be placed on his burial scaffold before Kefgawes, the Great Sun, reached the middle of the sky. His face would never be seen again, not even in the faces of his children. He had died so young that he had not yet fathered a child. So the women of his family cried and cried.

Hearing them cry, I wondered again why it was that men had to fight one another. I do not like war. Wars are like those Four Wind Giants. They only seek to eat the people.

10

JOHN SMITH

The Fort

Captain Newport, having always his eyes and ears open to the proceedings of the colony, 3 or 4 days before his departure, asked the president how he thought himself settled in the government—whose answer was that no disturbance could endanger him of the colony but it must be wrought either by Captain Gosnoll or Master Archer. For the one was strong with friends and followers, and could if he would; and the other was troubled with an ambitious spirit, and would if he could. The Captain gave them both knowledge of this the president's opinion, and moved them with many entreaties to be mindful of their duties to His Majesty and the colony.

—FROM A DISCOURSE OF VIRGINIA,
BY EDWARD MARIA WINGFIELD

MAY 26TH–JUNE 22ND, 1607

MANY NOW WERE the assaults and ambuscadoes of the salvages. We labored hard pallisadoing our fort which was built upon the western end of our point of land. Of his own accord, our worthy Captain Newport ordered his seamen to aid us. It was well that we set to work, for that Friday the salvages gave on again. This time, though, they came with more fear, daring not to come within musket range. Above forty arrows fell into and about the fort. They hurt not any of us, but finding one of our poor dogs, did kill him.

A quiet day followed. Then, upon Sunday, the first and thirtieth of May, they again came lurking in the thickets and tall grass. I had urged that we clear the land about the fort, but my words, as usual, had gone unheeded by the wisdom of the council. Eustace Clovell, a gentleman, was straggling unarmed outside the fort. The hidden salvages pierced him with six arrows in no more time than it does take to draw a breath. Wherewith Clovell came running into the fort.

"Arm, arm!" he cried loudly, those arrows sticking out of him and quivering as he ran.

The salvages stayed not, but ran away. Master Clovell himself departed after eight days of suffering from his grievous wounds.

On the very day of Clovell's death, two salvages came and presented themselves unarmed.

"Wingapo," they shouted.

I perceived them to be emissaries come from those kings with whom we had perfect league. But one of our gentlemen shot at them. As is their custom, the salvages fell down and then leaped up and ran away. Yet as they departed through the woods we heard them still crying *"wingapo"* withstanding.

Meanwhile, the building of our fort continued. Trenches were dug two feet deep. In them, heavy logs were placed side by side, strengthened by crosspieces, making a wall that rose high above our heads. Thus would we be well hidden from the spying eyes of any enemies. The shape of our fort was triangle-wise. The longest side, a full four hundred feet in length, lay upon the river, where our three ships were closely tied. Two hundred feet long were each of the other walls, with three bulwarks, like a half-moon, at every corner. In each bulwark were four or five pieces of mounted artillery. Truly we would make ourselves sufficently strong against any assault of the salvages.

What toil we had with so small a power to guard our work adays, watch all night, resist our enemies, and effect our business to relade the ships, cut down trees, and prepare the ground to plant our corn. We had but six weeks to spend in this manner. Captain Newport, who was hired only for our transportation, was to return with the ships.

Yet even in the midst of this toil and danger, much was the mischief that daily sprang from the ignorant yet ambitious spirits who hated John Smith. But the good doctrine and exhortation of our preacher Master Hunt reconciled them. For that, upon the tenth of June, I was released from confinement. Although some on that very day did yet protest and urge my punishment, I was set free without check.

Left hand upon the hilt of my sword, I stood forth before Master Hunt and the assembled company. Placing my right hand upon the Bible held out to me, I firmly spoke the words of the oath.

"I shall faithfully and truly declare my mind and opinion according to my heart and conscience in all things..."

As I spoke, my eyes sought those of the gentleman Wingfield. The brave Wingfield did not dare to meet them, but stared instead at the ground. The words of a piece of poetry then shaped themselves in my mind. I wrote them down that evening when there was pause between the work of labor and guard.

> Good men did ne'er their country's ruin bring
> But when evil men shall injuries begin,
> Not caring to corrupt and violate

The judgement seat for their own lucre's sake,
Then look, that country cannot long have peace,
Though for the present it have rest and ease.

Our men by their disorderly straggling were often hurt, when the salvages by the nimbleness of their heels well escaped. On the thirteenth of June, two of our mariners, Master John Collson and Master Mathew Fytch, foolishly went by themselves outside the wall. Eight salvages lay in wait among the weeds and tall grass. They shot Master Fytch dangerously in the breast and so ran away.

Upon the following day, the two salvages who had been driven off six days before again presented themselves unarmed and far beyond the range of our muskets. This time, recognizing one of them as a salvage who had shown kindness, I made sure that no shot was fired. They came in and certified to us who were friends and who foes, saying that the kings of Pamaunkee, Aratahec, Youghtamong, and Matapoll would aid us in making peace with our contracted enemies. Before they left, they counseled us to cut down the long weeds round about our fort. At that I permitted myself a smile.

◇·◆·◇·◆·◇

The fifteenth of June we had built and finished our fort. By the nineteenth, our ships were well laden with a great stock of shakes cut from the oaks and other trees. Such wood is of great value in trade, though we thought that the ore we had loaded was worth far more. The stone glittered with what certain of our company assured us was truly veins rich with gold. Little did we know then that our false gold was but antimony and those rocks worth no more than the weight of ballast. The true treasure of Virginia would never be in gold and silver, but in a simpler trade that only wise men would perceive.

The following day, June twentieth, all received the communion. Our church was a simple one. We hung an awning made from an old sail to three or four trees to shadow us from the sun. Our walls were rails of wood, our seats unhewed trees, our pulpit a bar of wood nailed to two neighboring trees. Rough though our cathedral was, surely God did most mercifully hear us—till the continued inundations of mistaking directions, factions, and numbers of unprovided libertines near consumed us all, as the Israelites in the wilderness.

The day following, the salvages voluntarily desire peace; and Captain Newport returned for England with news, leaving in Virginia the first planters, one hundred who knew not what sufferings lay ahead.

11

POCAHONTAS

❖◆❖◆❖◆❖◆❖◆❖◆❖◆❖◆❖

The Touch of a Woman's Hands

*After Great Hare drove the Four Wind Giants away, he made
the waters and in those waters placed the fish. Thus there
would be food in the waters for the people. Great Hare made
the plants of the earth, and on the earth he placed a Great
Deer. Great Deer fed upon those plants as Great Hare
intended.*

*The Four Wind Giants were still angry because Great
Hare had not allowed them to eat the first people. Now what
Great Hare had made caused them to be even more jealous. So
those Four Wind Giants came flying from their homes in the
four directions. They made spears from sharp poles. They
hunted the Great Deer and killed it with their spears. They
cut it into pieces and ate it, leaving only the hairs of the deer
scattered upon the ground. Then the Four Winds once more
went away.*

*Great Hare saw what the Four Wind Giants had done.
He gathered up all of the hairs of the Great Deer. Then Great
Hare began to chant and sing. As he sang and chanted, he
scattered the hairs of Great Deer on the earth. Each hair, when
it struck the earth, turned into a deer and ran away into the
forest. So it is that there are many deer to this day.*

I HAVE BEEN TOLD that there are not as many deer now in our land as there were when my father was my age. Utto-matomakkin has said that it may be that the deer are not pleased because we do not treat them with enough respect. So the leaders of the deer people have urged them to move away from our lands. It is the sort of thing that a priest would say.

Rawhunt thinks there are fewer deer just because there are more of our people here than there were when my father was a child. Rawhunt says that even though those sicknesses that seem to follow the Tassantassuk have spread through our land twice during his life, killing many people, still our people have survived, survived and grown in number, like the hairs of the deer scattered upon the earth. If a man would be a real man, he must be a good hunter, and so our men kill many deer each year.

I have watched the hunters bring the skins in tribute to my father. As the Great Chief, my father has a right to eight of every ten deerskins. He never takes that many, for if he did so it would make the people too poor and it would be hard for families to clothe themselves. But the men must bring those skins and lay them before him so that he can choose to take as many as he wishes. It reminds everyone of his power and of how strongly our alliance is bound together. If any village be-haves badly, my father may increase the number of skins he takes to punish its people.

◆◇◆◇◆

That story of Great Hare had come to me and made me go so deep into my thoughts that I forgot what I was supposed to do. It is that way when you are in the Moon Lodge, for it is a place that is meant to allow you to go deep into your thoughts.

"Pocahontas," Green Reed called from the other side of the Moon Lodge, "I am still waiting for you to bring me that deerskin to place over my lap."

I carefully chose a soft, smoke-tanned skin from the pile and brought it back to my elder mother.

I am not old enough to have my own moon time yet, but on this day I was being honored by those women who invited me to help them. They need such help, for when a woman spends her time in the Moon House each month—usually during those days and nights when Grandmother Moon is largest in the sky—that woman does no work herself. She does not cook or tan skins, she does not gather useful plants from the forest, or hoe in the gardens, or do any of the many, many things women must do so that the people can live well. At this time others must do the work, and she comes to stay here with her moon sisters in the special house at the edge of the village. She has nothing to do other than relax, and think, and talk. The younger women who do not yet have their moons bring food for her and do whatever small chores she asks them to do, whether it is to comb her hair or keep the fires burning.

I usually do much talking—some say too much. In the Moon Lodge, though, I mostly listen. So many things are always talked about by the women in the Moon Lodge. This day, many of those things had to do with the Coatmen.

Many of the things talked about in the Moon House become advice to reach the ears of Powhatan. It is true that my father is the Great Chief of our alliance, but his power does not just come from himself. It comes from his making the right decisions for the good of the people. It comes from the support and the advice of the women. Whenever he calls the people together in council, there are always women sitting beside him and behind him. We women often say that we know what a man will do long before he does it. After all, we are the ones who make up his mind for him.

"Are the Coatmen truly men?" Pemminawsqua motioned to me with her chin as she asked her question of the other women, who were gathered beside her in a circle.

I hurried over to hand her the scratching stick that she pointed at with her lips. When a woman is in her moon, she does not even scratch herself with her hands, but uses a special stick. Pemminawsqua is a very good-looking woman. Her arms and legs are round, her hips broad. She has four children and is a very good mother. I think my own birth mother would now look like her if she had lived. Pemminawsqua's face is also attractively round, round as Grandmother Moon, and it shines with health, smooth and lovely as the silk grass she is named for. She has a low, pleasant voice, and it seems as if she is close to a laugh whenever she speaks.

"I ask this," Pemminawsqua continued, "because they do not do the things that men are supposed to do."

"Or if they do them, they do them very poorly," Wighsakan agreed. "They are very poor hunters, they do not know how to find their way through the forest without becoming lost, and many of them seem to be cowards."

"This is true," Green Reed said. The way she said it meant she wanted to hear what the other, younger women had to say.

"They also do the things that women do," Atamasku, a thin woman with a high voice, said quickly. Of all the women who were in the Moon Lodge, Atamasku was the one who seemed the least relaxed. She is named for the lily that hides beneath the grass, but she is more like the hummingbird, who always wants to be in motion. "They are trying to plant corn and grow it," Atamasku said, patting her hands on her lap. "But the earth is not listening to them," she added, shaking not just her head, but her shoulders as well. "No. Nothing they have planted is growing well. Everyone knows the earth prefers the touch of a woman's hands."

"Ah," Pemminawsqua said in her soft voice. "But they have no women among them."

"Is it no wonder then that they are crazy?" Wighsakan said. "Who else but women can do what women do?" She smiled broadly and nodded to Pemminawsqua. "Truly, sister, the Coatmen do not even do the things that men do."

Everyone laughed for a long time because of what Wighsakan said.

Then, after a time of pleasant silence, the conversation turned to our own gardens. Although the women joked about the inability of the Coatmen to grow their crops, this had not been a good year for planting for our own crops. The dryness and the rains had come at the wrong times. Each year we plant four different crops of corn, two that usually ripen at the start of the summer, two more that come in the fall. This year our first harvest would be very small. If not for the many different kinds of food that we gather from the lands and waters, it could be hard for us when the crops do not grow well.

If the Coatmen are such bad hunters, I found myself thinking, *if they know so little about making crops grow, if they cannot find anything in the forest, if they have no women to show them the right way to live, how will they survive in the cold seasons?*

At that moment, even though I knew the Tassantassuk had been behaving very badly in many ways, I began to feel sorry for them.

12

JOHN SMITH

✦✧✦✧✦✧✦✧✦✧✦✧✦✧✦

The Hundred Left Behind

*The 22th, Captain Newport returned for England, for
whose good passage and safe return we made many prayers to
our Almighty God.*

*June the 25th, an Indian came to us from the Great
Poughwaton with the word of peace, that he desired greatly
our friendship, that the wyroaunces Paspaheigh and
Tapanough should be our friends, that we should sow and reap
in peace or else he would make wars upon them with us. This
message fell out true, for both those wyroaunces have ever
since remained in peace and trade with us. We rewarded the
messenger with many trifles, which were great wonders to him.*

—FROM A DISCOURSE OF VIRGINIA,
BY EDWARD MARIA WINGFIELD

JUNE 22ND–JULY 26TH, 1607

UPON THE MORNING of the second and twentieth of
June, Captain Newport departed in the *Susan Constant*
from James Port for England. His return was promised within
twenty weeks. Our store of food was only sufficient for three
months. Yet as I watched the sail of our Admiral grow small
and disappear, I misdoubted he would even that soon return.

"They shall come in time," said George Percy, as the last white billow vanished like the wing of a lost bird.

"All things come in time," I said, turning away from that doubtful sea. "But what time will that time be? I much mislike our circumstance."

So long had been spent in our crossing that our supplies were perilous low. There were still fish in the river, among them great sturgeon of seven or eight feet or more. Sea crabs, too, could be gathered from the waters. But our hunger was such that fishing night and day would not provide enough to feed the one hundred and four of us left behind. Already fewer fish were being caught. The mulberries and cherries and other fruits that we had seen in such profusion no longer could be found upon the bushes and trees close to James Fort. We dared not venture far from the fort for fear of the arrows of our foes. Bare and scanty of victuals were we and furthermore in war and danger of the salvages.

❖❖❖❖❖

On the five and twentieth, some good news came when a natural appeared at the edge of the clearing, making signs of peace and crying out, *"wingapo."* He revealed himself to be the emissary of the one he called the Great King, Powhatan. The other kings were bound to do the bidding of this greater one who wished our friendship. Although he would not yet come to us or allow us to visit him, the attacks upon our fort would now cease so that we might sow and reap in peace.

Good as this word was, that Great King sent us no gifts or corn or other food. Peace we had, but no less hunger. Each day was hotter than the last and the air almost too thick to breathe. Swarms of insects from the swamps, biting and buzzing gnats, came flocking about our faces, in such clouds that they sometimes filled our mouths as we breathed. The sweat and strain was great on those who would work. And now upon us came a host of sickness, fevers, swelling, and the bloody flux.

<hr/>

Being thus left to our fortunes, it soon fortuned that within ten days scarce ten men could either go or well stand, such extreme weakness and sickness oppressed us. And thereat none need marvel if they consider the cause and reason. While our ships stayed, our allowance had been somewhat bettered by a daily proportion of biscuits. The sailors pilfered both biscuits and drink from the ship's store to sell, give, or exchange with us for money, sassafras, or furs. But when they departed, there remained neither tavern, beer house, nor place of relief but the common kettle. We became so free of gluttony and drunkenness that all of us but our president might have been canonized as saints.

To himself our president engrossed a private hoard of oatmeal, sack, oil, aqua vitae, beef, eggs, and whatnot. All that he allowed equally to be distributed was half a pint of wheat and as much barley boiled with water for a man a day. This having fried some twenty and five weeks in the ship's hold, it contained as many worms as grains. Our drink was water, our lodging castles in the air.

Captain Bartholomew Gosnoll, my old and wise friend, clapped his hand upon my shoulder one day as I looked with worry at our state.

"Good John," he said, "our palisade has been well built. We are safe now."

As always, his gentle words were true enough and meant to bring peace. No natural could either see within nor breach our walls. I noted that our storehouse, too, was sturdily built.

Carefully guarded by our president, it was fashioned of pilings covered with clapboard, twigs, and mud, its roof a thatch of reeds gathered from the swamp. But now, weakened and lessened in numbers as we were, no further building could be done.

That evening in my tent, I shook my head as I read once again the *Instructions by Way of Advice* given us by the London Company for the making of our town: "*Set your houses even and by a line, that your streets may have a good breadth, and be carried square about your market place.*"

Wise and gentle words, indeed, but of little use when half the men were gentlemen unused to soiling their hands and even those disposed toward labor now grown too weak to work. I looked about our settlement and saw only tents grown grey and ragged from use and soldier holes dug into the earth. In these trenches, those more common and less fortunate slept covered by canvas and branches on the nights when the rains did not fill their shallow holes with water. Like graves those holes looked. And though there was little food in James Town, I thought that soon enough there would be graves aplenty.

13

POCAHONTAS

❖◦❖◦❖◦❖◦❖◦❖◦❖◦❖◦❖◦❖◦❖◦❖

The Strange Camp of the Coatmen

Now that Great Hare had placed the deer all throughout the land, he decided it was time to also release the people, for they could hunt the deer and thus survive on their own. So Great Hare opened his bag. Within that bag there were now many men and women. With care, Great Hare took them from his bag two by two. He placed a woman and a man in one country, then he placed another woman and man in another country and so on until there were people in every country. Those first people were the ancestors of all of us.

NEPINOUGH
TIME OF FIRST CORN HARVEST
LATE JUNE 1607

Now that I have seen the Coatmen, I have decided what I think of them. Rawhunt has decided that the Coatmen are fools. They seem to know how to do nothing, nothing right. Opechancanough, my father's youngest brother, says they are like ticks. Nothing but ticks. We must pluck the Tassantassuk from our flesh and crush them before they drink too much of our blood. My father, though, still suspects that the Coatmen may be of some use to him. I asked him when and how that might be. As always, he was patient in his answer to me.

"*Nechaun*," he said, "my child, it is like this. When you grasp a snake, you have to make sure you hold it firmly and in the right place. Otherwise it will twist around and bite you."

What do I think of the Coatmen? I think that though they are Outsiders, they are still human beings like ourselves, even if they are ignorant and foolish.

Perhaps I feel this sympathy because of who I am. I sometimes feel set apart from everyone, just as those foolish Coatmen must feel. They are so far from whatever land where their first mother and father lived. Because I am the favorite daughter of our Great Chief, I am allowed to sit close to him and listen in on his councils and see some of the great things he does. I also see how many fear him because of the great power he has held for so long. Because of that fear of my father's power, people treat me differently from other children. Even the friends I play with are more careful with me than with one another. Perhaps that is why I do so much teasing of others. It is a way of reminding people that I am a child, even if I am Powhatan's daughter.

I know that my father's power is not mine. When my father dies, that power will go to my uncle Opitchapam, his younger brother, who limps from an injury suffered as a child. Even if I were my father's son, I would not inherit his power. Among our people, power must always go first to the brothers before it goes to the sons.

Because my father is not a young man, the day when he takes the road to the house of the sunrise may come all too soon. True, many of our people live to see a hundred returnings of the leaves or even more. When a man or woman of our people has survived past the middle years, past the time of childbearing or warring to protect the people, they may be blessed with many more seasons. But, like many of our people, I am sometimes able to see things that are to come, and that ability to see what has not yet happened can be a little frightening. When I see myself as a grown woman, I do not see my father's face near me. I see myself walking with the Coatmen, but then that vision grows blurred, as if in a fog. Perhaps it is because we can never see ourselves clearly—either now or in the seasons to come.

I have thought of that vision often since seeing the Coatmen and their camp. Four days ago, my father finally agreed to allow me to make the journey. But he did not allow me to dress in my finery. When I started to turn away from him, in a hurry to get to my paint, he laughed and called me back to him.

"*Neamosens,* my daughter, there is no need to make yourself fine to look at when no one is going to see you," he said.

I could go and view their camp, he explained, but I could not approach it. He had just sent word to the Tassantassuk that they would no longer be under attack. He, Powhatan, had commanded it. Yet my father still did not trust those Coatmen. He had seen how ready they were to shoot their thunder weapons—even at those who tried to approach as friends.

"Your brother Naukaquawis and Rawhunt will go with you."

So Rawhunt and Naukaquawis and I, along with a party of younger men to guard us, crossed the river from my father's great town of Werowocomoco. We took the trail that led to the Tassantassuk camp. Although my legs are shorter than those of a grown man's, I kept up well. In fact, Naukaquawis had to keep calling me back whenever I got ahead of the others. I was so excited that I was as ready to run as a deer caught in a drive by the hunters. It was less than a day's journey. But I was so eager to see these strange men that it seemed as if many days had passed and the lazy sun had become stuck in the sky.

At last we neared the place. We approached from the land, not from the river side. The grass had been cut down all around their camp. We could see clearly all the way to the river, where two canoes bigger than any I had ever seen were tied to the big trees. The tide was high, so the canoes rocked with the gentle motions of the river. Big sticks, poles as big as trees, rose up from the two giant canoes. They did not have their white wings opened, but I saw that those tree-sized poles must be used to support their wings.

Those big canoes were strange and wonderful to see, even from a distance. The strangest thing I saw, though, were the two cornfields. It was not just how badly planned and planted they were. The soil there would never be good for a crop of corn. It was too marshy and salty. What was truly strange was to see men, grown men, working in those fields, trying to hoe and weed as women do. It was such a foolish sight. Of course they were doing it all wrong. They also were dressed in so much clothing that I could see how uncomfortable they were, especially in the great heat of the sun. It made me want to laugh, but I kept quiet.

Naukaquawis tapped me on the shoulder and gestured with his chin toward one part of the tall wall of logs built all around the Coatmen's strange camp. There was an opening there. A man stood in front. He was holding the longest spear I had ever seen, guarding the entrance to their town. But he was not a very good guard. He had not seen us at all.

Two young men from Paspahegh had joined us as we came close to the Coatmen's camp. There are always a few of them keeping watch on the Tassantassuk. Of course, they knew who Naukaquawis and I were. They were treating us with great respect, as they certainly should. But they were also finding it hard to keep from joking about the foolishness of the Coatmen.

"I do not know why we are crouching down like this," the

first of the Paspahegh men said. "The Coatmen are so blind that they would not see us if we stood up and waved at them."

"Just be grateful that the wind is blowing away from us," said the second Paspahegh. "Otherwise we would be choking from the scent of those skunks!"

"It is true," Rawhunt said, "it is true. Wait until the wind changes. Just wait."

We were so far away from the stockade and the fields that Naukaquawis and I thought those words were only teasing. But then the breeze did shift, as it often does when the tides change. It blew up from the river, bringing us the smell of the salt and the marsh, rotting grass and dead fish. But that was not all we smelled. The rank odor of dirty clothing and men who washed even less than they cleaned their clothes also came to us. It was so strong that it was funny. Choking with laughter, my brother and I turned away from the camp of the Coatmen and followed Rawhunt back up the trail toward home.

14

JOHN SMITH

✦❖✦❖✦❖✦❖✦❖✦❖✦❖✦❖✦❖✦❖✦

The Sickness Time

The 3 of July, 7 or 8 Indians presented the president a deer from Pamaonoke, a wyroaunce desiring our friendship. They inquired after our shipping, which the president said was gone to Croatoon. They fear much our ships, and therefore he would have them think it not far from us. Their wyroaunce had a hatchet sent him; they were well contented with trifles.

A little after this came a deer to the president from the Great Powhatan. He and his messengers were pleased with the like trifles. The president likewise bought divers times deer of the Indians, beavers and other flesh, which he always caused to be equally divided amongst the colony.

About this time divers of our men fell sick; we missed above forty before September did see us.

—from A Discourse of Virginia,
by Edward Maria Wingfield

JULY 27TH–SEPTEMBER 5TH, 1607

O UR EXTREME LABOR in bearing and planting pallisados had strained and bruised us. Our continual toil in the extremity of the heat had weakened us. None, save our president, escaped want or sickness. Like all the others, I, too, became ill. But the many years spent in travel and at war had strengthened me far beyond those whose only labor had been the lifting of a finger to bid a servant wait upon them. I was among the first to regain health. By my good care, Martin and Ratliffe were preserved and relieved. Most of the soldiers recovered with the skillful diligence of Master Thomas Wotton, our chirugeon general.

My friend, the good and simple George Percy, was among those who survived this time of sickness. Though a gentleman, he never feared toil and was in dismay at our sorry state.

As he and I stood beside the river, Percy gestured toward those of our company who were dipping water. They did so like men half-asleep, not even troubling to brush aside the green scum which coated the surface.

"It is full of slime and filth now," Percy said, "yet when the tide is at flood it is very salt. With no other drink than this is it any wonder that we sicken?"

I nodded. I also bethought myself of the aqua vitae and communion wine which had vanished into the care of the president.

The eyes of the forest were upon us. So our timid president ordered us to stay always close to the walls. Though there would be food aplenty further afield and springs of fresh water there, too, we might be found by the arrows of the naturals. From May to September, we lived upon sturgeon and sea crabs. But our nets which once brought up four or five fish at a cast now caught fewer and fewer fish.

On the sixth of August, John Asbie died of the bloody flux. It was the beginning of a sad toll that brings tears to the eye yet to tell it. On the ninth died John Flower of the swelling. On the tenth, William Brewster, gentleman, of a wound given by the salvages. The fourteenth day, Jerome Alikock, ancient, died of a wound; the same day, Francis Midwinter and Edward Moris, corporal, died suddenly. The fifteenth day, Edward Browne and Stephen Galthorpe; the sixteenth day, Thomas Gower, gentleman; the seventeenth day, Thomas Mounslic; the eighteenth, Robert Pennington, gentleman; the nineteenth died Drue Piggase, gentleman.

Good Captain Bartholomew Gosnoll had questioned the wisdom of planting our colony in this place, preferring that point of land Master Archer most modestly named "Archer's Hope." The soil there was good and there was great store of vines, many animals and birds. Our president and the other members of the council had disliked it because the ship could not ride so near the shore, though we might have settled there to the contentment of all. Despite this disagreement, and our president's jealousy, Captain Gosnoll had yet remained a voice of reason. He never sought to overthrow, but only to give counsel. All men admired him for his kindness and wisdom. Even such plotters as Master George Kendall, who worked to sow discontent, grew silent when Gosnoll spoke his calming words.

On the fifth of August, Gosnoll himself grew ill. Despite the efforts of our chirugeon, his condition worsened each day. I begged that his ration of food be increased, that he be given such wine as might yet remain.

"Our rations must remain the same," President Wingfield replied, puffing his chest out like a virtuous pigeon and allowing none to enter his house, where the stores of food were jealously guarded. "Every man shall have his portion according to his place. There is no wine to be had. We cannot favor the sick over those who are well, even those who are your favorites. I will not yield to your warrants."

I marked those words, as well as the fact that the earth was disturbed in the president's tent, as if something had been hastily buried there. I went then and sat by the bedside of Captain Gosnoll, who had drawn me into this enterprize. I held the hand of the good old man and spoke to him of the fine times that would yet come, of how fair this land of Virginia yet might be for us all.

"Upon your life," I said, "stands a great part of the good success and fortune of our government and colony."

So weak had that worthy and religious gentleman become that he could only squeeze my hand. I turned aside that I might not show the tears in my eyes.

On the two and twentieth of August, there died Captain Bartholomew Gosnoll, the best of those on our council. He was honorably buried, having all the ordnance in the fort shot off with many volleys of small shot.

From that day on things happened fast and furious. Both night and day the air was filled with the groans, the pitiful murmurings, and outcries of sick men in every corner of the fort. The names of the dead now grew too many for my weary memory to list. Many times three and four a night would perish and their bodies would be dragged out of their cabins like dogs. We buried them in graves dug as deep as we might go in the soggy earth within the walls of our fort so that the naturals might not view the lessening of our numbers. We now had no more than five able men at any time strong enough to stand and man the bulwarks.

There is no doubt that we all would have perished had it not been for the grace of God, who sent those people who were our mortal enemies to bring us corn, bread, fish, and flesh. Those gifts of God, delivered by the hands of the naturals, set up our feeble men.

Even in our weakness, there were still some with strength to plot and plan.

"We shall die here," Kendall whispered to those he thought would heed him. "We can overthrow the council, seize the *Discovery*, and sail away from this cursed land of Virginia."

Those words of revolt reached the ears of myself and the others of the council. We were quick to act. Kendall was removed from the council. Since he so wished to go on the *Discovery*, I saw that he was placed there upon the ship, in irons and under guard.

15

POCAHONTAS

◆◈◆◈◆◈◆◈◆◈◆◈◆◈◆◈◆◈◆◈◆

Corn

Although the corn, like all good things, was made by Ahone, it is said that corn was not owned by all the people at first. Those who lived in the direction of the Summer Land owned the corn and did not share it. Kahgah, the Great Crow, saw this and decided that it was not right. So Kahgah stole the corn from the South people. Great Crow flew from village to village, dropping kernels of corn for all the people to plant.

Because Kahgah, the Great Crow, brought the corn, all the crows think that they have a right to eat as much corn as they want. So when the corn first begins to ripen, many crows come flying in to take their share of the harvest. That is why our children have to keep watch on the fields to protect the corn. They make noise and wave their arms and throw sticks to drive those hungry crows away. If they did not do so, the great-grandchildren of Kahgah would take all the corn.

But because we remember who first brought corn to the people, we always leave some in the fields after the harvest so that Kahgah's great-grandchildren may have a share.

THE WOMEN AND children have been busy all day with the harvest of my father's gardens. To plant and care for the fields of the Great Chief is one of the duties our people owe to him as Mamanatowic. All are glad to do this, just as they do not mind bringing all of the skins of the deer to my father so that he may take the share he is owed. They know how hard their lives might be if it were not for the power of Powhatan.

Our villages are surrounded by enemies in three directions. If my father had not brought us together, we might have been destroyed. Even with his power, there is still danger from those enemy people who do not speak our language. They want to take women and children as captives and drive us from our fields and hunting and fishing places. But it is well known that the men of our villages are strong warriors. They are unafraid and are seldom defeated in battle. Even when they are taken as prisoners, they sing their death songs and refuse to show the enemy any sign of weakness. They will answer my father's call whenever it is necessary to go to war against the enemies.

Now and then the Monacanuk and Mannahoacuk, who live in the direction of the sunset, test our strength with raids. The Massawomeckuk and the Pocoughtaonackuk watch us from the direction of the Winter Land like hungry wolves. Then there is the newer danger of those Tassantassuk, who come upon us from the direction of the water with their powerful thunder weapons. However, those new ones huddled in their little stockade do not seem that dangerous to me, especially since their big swan canoe left.

Because of my father's strength, our villages can harvest the fields without the constant fear of war. It is not hard work, because all work together. As my oldest mother, Green Reed, says, what one hand finds hard to lift is lighter than a feather when many lift together. People love the time of the late summer harvest with its songs and joking.

True, everyone also looks forward to the time when the berries are ripe. Cattapeuk, the season when the leaves form, is a hungry one. Our winter stores have been used up, and everyone has grown thin. When the berry time comes, there is enough food in the forest for people to start to again grow fat. But it seems that everyone agrees that the season of harvest is the very best of all. I know that there is no time I love better than this. Even though, as the favorite daughter of the Mamanatowic, I do not have to work hard with my hands like the other children of my age, I go into the fields and take part in the harvest. People smile when they see me helping. Sometimes they tease me.

"Look," they say. "The One Who Makes Mischief has come among us to help. Give her the heaviest basket to carry."

Of course they do not do that. But they let me help as much as I want to. Sometimes, though, I like to just stand there in the field. The wind moves the long leaves of the corn plants and they caress my face. I say a quiet thank-you to the spirit of the corn for returning another harvest to us. As everyone knows, it is always important to express your thanks to the food plants, or they may fail to bring forth a good harvest the next time. Then I reach out and pick an ear of corn. The smell and feel of new ears of corn are so good. I like to pull back the husk and eat the green corn right from the ear, feeling its juice run down my cheeks.

❖·❖·❖·❖

People are already boiling some of the green ears of corn. When they have boiled enough, the corn will be stirred in with beans and cooked together to make *pausarowmena*. From now on, through the winter, there will always be a pot of *pausarowmena* in every home. Everyone has their own wooden spoon that they carry with them, usually hung from their belt on a rawhide cord with a toggle on it. You are welcome to enter any lodge whose door is open and dip in your spoon to help yourself to food from that pot. No one goes hungry among us as long as there is food in our homes. The visitor is just as welcome to share that food as is the dearest member of the family.

I wonder if the Tassantassuk share food as we do. Now that we have so much from our harvest, corn and squash and beans, we will be able to trade it with them. I am sure that they would like to have some of our harvest. I have heard that the Tassantassuk now look thin and hungry and that they move like sick men. Maybe, if they are polite to us, we will just give them food.

16

JOHN SMITH

❖❖❖❖❖❖❖❖❖❖❖❖❖❖❖❖❖❖❖❖❖

Deposed

Thus we lived for the space of five months in this misrable distress, not having five able men to man our bulwarks upon any occasion. If it had not pleased God to put a terror in the savages' hearts, we had all perished by those wild and cruel pagans, being in that weak estate we were, our men night and day groaning in every corner of the fort, most pitiful to hear. . . .

It pleased God after a while to send those people who were our mortal enemies to relieve us with victuals, as bread, corn, fish, and flesh in great plenty, which was the setting up of our feeble men, otherwise we had all perished. Also we were frequented by divers kings in the country bringing us a store of provisions to our great comfort.

The eleventh day, there was certain articles laid against Master Wingfield. . . .

—FROM OBSERVATIONS GATHERED OUT OF
A DISCOURSE OF THE PLANTATION OF THE SOUTHERN COLONY
IN VIRGINIA BY THE ENGLISH, 1606.
WRITTEN BY THAT HONORABLE GENTLEMAN,
MASTER GEORGE PERCY.

DESPITE THE GIFTS of food brought by the naturals, all still suffered greatly from hunger. It made it not easier when our president, in his wisdom, ordered that for every meal of fish or flesh we enjoyed, we would be denied our allowance of porridge. This was as true for the sick as it was for the whole. In despair, despite their fears of how the naturals might treat them, some of our men went runagate into the wilderness.

On the sixth of September, the werowance of Paspihae sent back to us Richard Mutton, one of our boys who had run off. Our brave president, on seeing the boy missing four days before, had assured us that he would never be seen again.

"It is known," said Wingfield, "that the salvages are cannibals. Mutton he was and mutton he now is most certainly."

Instead, the naturals had fed the boy and treated him so kindly that he had begged to remain with them. But Paspihae brought him back as an assurance of his peace with us.

Though they often touched him and stroked his hair, no salvage had treated him cruelly. But our president did not spare him four strokes of the rod across his shoulders, one for each day of his desertion.

As young Richard sat nursing his stripes and huddled with the other boys, I overheard him telling them of his experiences.

"The men and women," Mutton whispered, "do not seem to hardly work at all, but they have aplenty of vittles to eat. They spend most of the night in singing or howling. Every morning they carry all the little children to the river's sides, but what they do there I do not know."

The other werowances did, like Paspihae, send back our men who had run off to them. Each of them was used well during their being with the naturals. But each man was so well rewarded with the rod—as had been young Richard—upon his return home, that it was assured each would take little joy to travel abroad without passport.

Now, their second harvest having come in, the naturals began to bring corn and flesh to us daily. In three weeks, more than twenty men had reared up able to work. Strength to work also brought us strength to make protest against the despotical practices of our president.

Those of us in the council went to the president to beg for better allowances, especially for the sick.

"I will not be partial," Wingfield replied, closing the trunk which had been open as we entered his tent. He then wiped something which looked much like a bit of conserve from his mouth and continued his righteous discourse. "If one had any-thing of me, every man shall have his portion according to his place. I shall grant no larger allowance to you or your privates. Were I to enlarge the proportion according to your requests, in a short time I would starve the whole company."

Then the gentle Wingfield looked down his long nose upon us. A look came over his face like that of a pig that thinks itself a fox. He raised his hands to the sky and then placed them upon his ample bosom.

"I would gladly give up my office. Indeed, I would earnestly urge you to bestow the presidency upon some other, for I would prefer to be a private man. Yet I cannot do so, for I am pledged to do His Majesty good service."

That night, Ratliffe and Martin and I resolved that action must be taken. If we did not act, others would surely do so. Gabriell Archer had brought to us a paper-book loaded full of articles against the president. No man or boy, it seemed, was without his just complaint. Even my friend Percy, who is honest yet also thick like unto a post, voiced his agreement. Therefore we drew up certain articles in writing and took our oaths upon the Evangelists to observe them.

On the tenth of September, we went to the president's tent.

"We have here a warrant to depose the president," we told him. "He has proven himself unworthy to be either president or of the council. Therefore we discharge him of both and appoint John Ratliffe the new president."

Again that look of low cunning came over the face of Wingfield as he stood before us. It seemed he had expected this, for he held the charter in his hands.

"You would ease me," he said, "of a great deal of care and trouble. Yet the president may not be removed, as appeareth in Our Majesty's instructions for our government, except by the greater number of the voices of twelve councilors. You are but three. Thus I may not give up my office."

I shook my head. "If we do you wrong," I said, "then we must answer for it. You are president no longer."

With a readiness that was itself suspicious, Wingfield spread wide his hands.

"I am at your pleasure," he said, a serpent's smile upon his thick lips. "Dispose of me as you will without further garboil."

17

POCAHONTAS

Punishment

It is the job of our warriors to protect the people. We remember it at this time of the year whenever we look up into the sky. There we see in the stars the shape of Manguahaian, the Great Bear.

Long ago, they say, Manguahaian lived and walked upon the earth. Great Bear was so large that he could swallow a lodge with one gulp. He was a great danger to the people, who feared that he would destroy us all. Among us in those days there were four warriors who were great hunters. In the season of Taquitock, when the leaves fall, they promised that they would punish Great Bear, kill or drive him away so that the people would be safe. The quiyoughsokuk *made circles of cornmeal and sprinkled grains of corn to see what Okeus would tell them. They read the message that these four warriors would be successful as long as they never gave up but always continued on until they had succeeded.*

So those men sprinkled tobacco on the pawcorance, *the sacred stone at the edge of their village. They washed themselves in the river as the sun rose and set out. Soon they found the giant footprints of the Great Bear. Seeing them coming, Great Bear became afraid and began to run, and the four warriors followed.*

Great Bear ran upriver to the place where the land rises
and becomes rocky. The four warriors stayed close behind.
Great Bear reached the mountains and began to climb, hoping
to lose the hunters. But they continued on.

The day ended, but they ran on by the light of the moon.
They climbed higher, where flakes of snow sparkled on the dark
mountain. At last, Great Bear began to tire. The hunters came
close enough to throw their spears and killed him.

Then one of them looked around. The lights of many fires
sparkled all around them. Far below them was the earth. They
had chased Great Bear up into the Sky Land, among the stars.

"Look," one of the hunters shouted, "Manguahaian is alive
again."

They turned and saw that Great Bear had risen to his feet
and was running. The four hunters took up the pursuit once
more. To this day, if you look up into the night sky you will see
them. At Taquitock they strike Great Bear with their spears.
He falls on his back, and his blood colors the leaves. But every
year he rises again and runs, and faithful to their promise, the
four warriors follow.

TAQUITOCK
TIME OF HARVEST
EARLY SEPTEMBER

IT IS IMPORTANT for us to keep our promises. It has always
been that way among our people. One of my father's hard
jobs is to punish those who do not keep their promises. Because
he has the power to order someone punished—or even killed if
the person has done a great wrong—my father is feared. I do
not think he enjoys this job, but he has done it for many years
and I have heard people saying that he is fair. (I have heard them
saying this when they have not known I was listening to them.)

I have also seen people being punished. I did not want to watch, but my father told me that I should do so and that I should show no emotion or pity. That was very hard for me to do, for I do not like to see any person suffering. I watched as a man who often mistreated his wife was told to kneel before my father. Everyone was told what the man had done and reminded that all those who behaved in this way would suffer the same punishment. Then Uttomatomakkin beat the man with a stick. The man did not flinch or cry out, even though he was struck many times. When it was done, the man who had been punished stood and swore that he would never again do such a bad thing. Although I was not happy to watch, in the end it made me proud to see him behave as a man should behave.

Another of the bad things that requires harsh punishment is stealing from our own people. That is such a selfish thing, as selfish as not sharing your food with those of our people who are hungry. (Although my father, as Mamanatowic, always has greater stores of grain than anyone else, whenever there is a poor harvest, he makes certain that food is given out to all who need it.) A man or woman whose heart is greedy, who steals from his own people, is as worthless as a cracked pot. Just as water spills from a cracked pot so, too, honor leaks from a person who steals.

If someone is caught stealing three times, that person will be killed. The thief's death will not be an honorable one, of the sort that is given to enemy warriors taken in battle. During that kind of slow execution, a brave person is given the chance to prove their courage by not crying out or begging for mercy. Instead, someone who is a constant thief will be punished in just the same way one is punished for murdering one of our own people. That person will be thrown down on the great flat *pawcorance* and clubbed to death.

I have never watched anyone being executed. Even if someone deserves to die, my heart does not wish to see it. I think that I would try to stop it if I were forced to be present, even if the person was guilty of so terrible a crime as having a heart so selfish and twisted that he would steal from his own.

By stealing, I do not mean taking things from our enemies or from the Tassantassuk. When one is brave or clever enough to go into the village of an enemy nation and take something from them, that is not a bad thing. When the Coatmen first arrived, many of our people were clever enough to take many things from them. I know this because those things were always brought straight to my father. Taking things to give to the Mamanatowic is a very honorable thing, a deed that someone can brag about. Those who give them know that my father will use those items for the good of our people. So our people have obtained fine knives and beautiful jewelry to wear and even a few of the Coatmen's pots that do not break. The Tassantassuk are very careless. It almost seems as if they want to have their fine things stolen from them.

The one thing, though, that my father most wants no one has yet been able to steal. He wants some of the Coatmen's thunder sticks. But they are very cautious about guarding their weapons.

"It may be," I have heard my father say, "that the only way I will be able to get some of those new weapons will be to make their leader into one of my werowances. Then, because I will be his Great Chief, he will have to keep his promise to obey me and give me what I ask for."

18

JOHN SMITH

Trial

I will now write what followeth in my own name and give the new president his title. I shall be the briefer, being thus discharged.

I was committed to a sergeant and sent to the pinnace, but I was answered with if they did me wrong they must answer it.

The 11th of September, I was sent to come before the president and council upon their court day.

They had now made Master Archer recorder of Virginia. The president made a speech to the colony that he thought it fit to acquaint them why I was deposed. I am now forced to stuff my paper with frivolous trifles, that our grave and worthy council may the better strike those veins where the corrupt blood lieth, and that they may see in what manner of government the hope of the colony now travaileth.

—FROM A DISCOURSE OF VIRGINIA,
BY EDWARD MARIA WINGFIELD

SEPTEMBER 11TH, 1607

I THANK GOD THAT I have never undertaken anything yet for which any could tax me of carelessness or dishonesty.

Seeing our former president on trial was a sad lesson for those who would value the state of his own belly above that of the general good. Yet so full of himself was Master Wingfield that he still puffed himself up one moment and the next looked to the heavens like one who has been wronged.

Each on the council voiced his reasons for deposing the former president. John Ratliffe stood with a small bag in his hand and spoke of how Wingfield had refused even the smallest necessities.

"I asked him for a pennywhittle and he denied it to me," Ratliffe said. "Whether my request was that one of the chickens he claimed were his and his alone be given to the common pot or that he grant me but a spoonful of beer, his answer was always a refusal. Instead, he served me with a handful of foul corn."

With that our new President reached into the bag, held up a handful of that corn which was grey and crawling with maggots, and then cast it down upon the earth.

To this, Master Wingfield's sole reply was to sigh like an innocent, then open wide his hands and turn his gaze to the sky. He ignored the muttering of the crowd of men who all had been given their own handfuls of such spoiled victuals by the generous gentleman.

I was next. I aimed my words not at greed, but at his haughtiness.

"He has called me a liar," I said. "He has said that though we are equal here, if he were in England he would think it scornful to make me his companion."

I waited to see if Wingfield would again repeat his own lie, that I had gone as a beggar around Ireland. He did not.

Captain John Martin then spoke. Master Martin is not only a ship's captain, his father is the Master of the Mint and

Lord Mayor of London. This was a gentleman upon whom the gentle Wingfield could not look down.

Captain Martin leaned close to Wingfield, staring him in the eye until Wingfield was forced to turn his own gaze to the ground.

"This man," Martin growled, "is no man at all. He has done slack service in our colony. Indeed, he does nothing but tend his own pot, spit, and oven." Martin clenched his fist and his face grew red. "He hath starved my son and denied him a spoonful of beer. I have friends in England shall be revenged on him, if ever he come to London."

Master Wingfield's own face paled, but seeing Captain Martin take his seat, he took courage.

"Should I answer these complaints?" he drawled. "Or is there aught to charge me withal?"

At that, President Ratliffe pulled out the paper-book loaded with articles against him and gave them to Archer to read.

"Master President," Wingfield protested, "by the instruction of our government, our proceedings ought to be verbal, not written. I desire a copy of these articles and time to answer them likewise in writing."

"That will not be granted," President Ratliffe replied in a voice as cold as stone. But some thought now began to pass through his head. Archer had not read half the complaints before our new president raised his hand.

"Stay, stay," Ratliffe said. "We know not whether he will abide our judgement or appeal to the King. How say you, sir? Will you appeal to the King or no?"

A smile now appeared on Master Wingfield's face, seeing himself thus plucked out of the fire.

At the same time a murmur began to grow among the gentlemen in the crowd.

"If others would join me," Richard Crofts said in a voice whose calm made it no less threatening, "I would not just pull him out of his seat, but out of his skin!"

"Master President," Wingfield cried, "His Majesty's hands are full of mercy and I do appeal to them."

"So shall it be," President Ratliffe replied, raising his hand even higher as he looked about the circle of angry faces. Some there would gladly have seen Master Wingfield shot or skinned, but I stood beside the President, my hand held close to the butt of my French pistol. The murmurs soon subsided.

Ratliffe nodded. He gestured to the master of the pinnace and then pointed at Wingfield's fat belly. "Look to him well. He is now the King's prisoner."

Thus it came to be that Master Wingfield and the mutinous Kendall were placed together. Yet, though living in disgrace on the pinnace, they still sought to strengthen themselves with the sailors and other confederates to regain their former credit and authority. More trouble was soon to come.

19

POCAHONTAS

Trade

Among our people, all of the men pluck out the hair on the right side of their head, wearing it long only on the left side. Long ago, before our men learned to do this, they wore their hair long on both sides. Sometimes their long hair would tangle in their bowstrings. Then Okeus took the shape of a man and appeared to the quiyoughsokuk. *Even though he was in the shape of a person, they recognized him as a god. They saw that there was no hair on the right side of his head and that the long hair on the left side of his head was bound into a knot with the horn of a deer thrust through it.*

"This is the proper way for a man," Okeus said to them. "This is the way it should be for all men from this time on."

TAQUITOCK
TIME OF HARVEST
MID-SEPTEMBER 1607

M Y UNCLE OPECHANCANOUGH has begun to wonder if any of the Tassantassuk are real men.

"Hunh!" he said. "It is not only that they wear their hair as women do. They also do the work of women."

"Badly," Amocis replied with a smile. Amocis is as clever as a fox. He is like the hungry fox who watches and listens, waiting for that moment when the rabbit is so foolish that he comes close enough to be caught. That is why my father uses him to gather information. Yet even my father has said that he does not fully trust Amocis as he does Nauriaus. Nauriaus has been able to keep a close watch on the Tassantassuk when they have used him as a guide and has brought my father much useful information.

My uncle Opechancanough laughed at what Amocis said. Of all my uncles, Opechancanough is the one who likes most to laugh. He is also acknowledged by everyone to be the bravest of warriors. Brave as he is, he is not as patient as my father. If my uncle were Mamanatowic, he would have wiped out the Tassantassuk by now.

As soon as he finished laughing at Amocis's words, my uncle's face grew serious again. "Those Coatmen also show no courage. They go about like beggars, asking for food. They do not know how to show hospitality in return when our people visit them. Instead, they scream like little boys who have not yet been killed and brought back to life as men. They are all afraid of us. Hunh! Have you not seen how they step back in fear whenever one of our men teases them or bullies them to see what they will do? If they did not have their thunder weapons, they would run from us like deer before a party of hunters."

Amocis smiled again and swung his hand down toward the ground. "They are not deer," he said. "They live inside the walls of their stockade in holes dug into the ground, like woodchucks."

Opechancanough began to laugh again. "Hunh, they are as hairy as the woodchuck. Maybe that is what they really are. Woodchucks who have learned to walk upright and act like human beings."

"Your words are wise," Amocis said. His face became serious. "What you say is true of most of the Coatmen. But their

Captain Newport, the one-handed werowance, he behaved as a man and a leader."

"Unh-hunh." My uncle rubbed his chin with his hand. "That is true. He also spoke some of our words, as a man should. But now he is gone, taking with him the two great *quintansuk* with swan wings. Maybe he left because he was so disgusted with what cowards the rest of them are. Amocis, *nettoppew*, have you seen any of them who behave as if they are real men?"

Amocis held up his little finger. *"Necut,"* he said. "There is at least one. The little angry one with the red hair on his face."

My uncle rubbed his chin again. *"Kator,"* he said. "You speak truly. I think I would like to talk to that one."

From what I have heard, it does seem as if the Tassantassa that we call Little Red-Haired Warrior is the bravest of the Coatmen. Over the last few days, he has begun to go up and down the river in the one remaining swan canoe, the smallest of the three. Like all the Tassantassuk, he is always hungry. We now have a song about them that is very funny.

> *Whe Whe Tassantassuk,*
> *always hungry, always begging*
> *Whe whe Tassantassuk*
> *ya ha ha ne he ho*

One day, Little Red-Haired Warrior went looking for food all the way to Kecoughtan. When he reached there, Amocis told me, the people did not want to trade with him. They were disgusted with the strange behavior of the Coatmen. They were also angry because some of their men had been wounded by the thunder weapons two seasons ago when the strangers first arrived. Because of what had happened, when the big swan canoe pulled up to shore this time and the Coatmen fired their thunder weapons, all of the people retreated from them. The old ones and the women and children went and hid in the forest. But the forty warriors of Kecoughtan had a plan. They did not run away. They went into the *yihacan* of Okeus and made themselves ready. They painted themselves black and white and red and placed Okeus on a platform so that they could carry him with them into battle. They were sure that the Tassantassuk would see the fearsome power of Okeus and run away. The Okeus of Kecoughtan is not as frightening or dangerous as the one in my father's village, or so I have been told. But I still would not like to look at him. At Kecoughtan the spirit of Okeus is held inside a shape almost as large as a man, made of skins stuffed with moss and covered with copper and necklaces of shells. Only the most fearless of men have the courage to touch him or carry him into battle.

As soon as the men of Kecoughtan left the *yihacan* of Okeus, they began to sing one of their war songs. They stomped their feet as they sang and made a sound that should have terrified the Tassantassuk as they came out of the village toward the beach. The air shook with the power of their song.

But Little Red-Haired Warrior was leading the Coatmen that day. He did not run. He stood calmly, stroking the hair on his face. His seven men stood behind him. When the men of Kecoughtan were only a spear's throw away, Little Red-Haired Warrior made his thunder weapon spit fire over the heads of the Kecoughtans, and his seven men did the same with their weapons. The sound of their thunder was so loud that it killed the war song the men of Kecoughtan had been chanting. The legs of those who carried Okeus became too weak to hold them up, and the men fell on the ground. The other warriors of Kecoughtan fled.

That Little Red-Haired Warrior showed such courage was a good thing. What he did next was even better. He and his men did not try to steal food, even though baskets of corn lay all around the village. They did not strike the men who lay on the ground. They did not take away the image of Okeus or try to damage him as an enemy would. Instead, he and his men simply stood and waited. Finally the *quiyoughsokuk* of Kecoughtan came out of the *yihacan* of Okeus and approached them.

Little Red-Haired Warrior gestured for him to come closer. He placed his hand on his heart to show he would be a friend and made other signs indicating that he wanted to trade for food. If six men would come forth and load their boat with corn, he would give them beads, copper, and hatchets.

This pleased the people of Kecoughtan, just as it pleased me when I heard Amocis tell of Little Red-Haired Warrior's actions. It pleased them even more when they saw how kind he was to the little children who began to gather around him. He allowed them to touch him and his strange clothing. He gave them gifts.

It makes me smile when I see this in my mind, when I close my eyes and watch my Little Red-Haired Warrior behaving like a true human being with our people. It was how a true warrior should behave, stern to those who would fight with him but gentle with those who are weak, and kind to those who would be friends. That is why when our men go to fight they are careful never to injure women and children or those too old to fight. In the same way, they show honor to the werowances and their families. When werowances or any of their families are captured in battle, they are never injured or tortured but brought back to be held as honored captives.

Soon the people of Kecoughtan were giving food to the Tassantassuk. They made a great feast of venison and turkeys, squash and *ponepope*. They brought bowls of *pausarowmena* and cups of *puccahiccora*. As the Tassantassuk left, Little Red-Haired Warrior was smiling. He stood in the front of their swan canoe and waved his hand at the people on the beach as they sang and danced in sign of their friendship.

20

JOHN SMITH

❖❖❖❖❖❖❖❖❖❖❖❖❖

Treason

Item: The English in that country have among themselves proclaimed and sworn the King of England as King of Virginia. And the anxiety they feel that the secrets of this country shall not be known, is so great that they have issued orders prohibiting anyone from taking letters with him beyond the frontiers, and also from sending any, except to private individuals, without their first being seen and read by the governor. For the same reason they have tried in that fort of theirs at Jamestown an English captain, a Catholic, called Captain Tindol, because they knew that he had tried to get to Spain, in order to reveal to His Majesty all about this country and many plans of the English which he knew, but which the narrator does not know.

—Report of what Francisco Maguel, an
Irishman, learned in the state of Virginia
during the eight months he was there.
(From an enclosure in a letter from Don
Alonso de Velasco, the Spanish Ambassador
in London, to the King of Spain)

SEPTEMBER 17TH, 1607–NOVEMBER 28TH, 1607

T HE NEW PRESIDENT and Martin were little beloved, of
weak judgement in dangers, and even less industrious in

peace. So it was that they committed the managing of all things to me. I knew that I must spare no pains to make homes for the company, who, notwithstanding our misery, little ceased their malice, grudging, and muttering. It seemed they would rather starve and rot with idleness than be persuaded to do anything for their own relief without constraint. By my own good example, good words, and fair promises I set some to mow, others to bind thatch, some to build houses and others to thatch them. Myself always bearing the greatest task for my own share, in short time I provided them lodgings, neglecting any for myself.

This done, I was constrained to be cape merchant and sent to the mouth of the river to Kecoughtan, an Indian town, to trade for corn and try the river for fish. Our fishing we could not effect by reason of the stormy weather. At Kecoughtan they scorned me at first as a famished man. In derision they offered me a handful of corn and a piece of bread for our swords and muskets. Seeing that by trade and courtesy there was nothing to be had, I made bold to try such conclusions as necessity enforced. So I let fly my muskets and ran my boat on shore, whereat they all fled into the woods.

God, the absolute disperser of all hearts, then altered their conceits. Now they became no less desirous of our commodities than we of their corn. With fish, bread, oysters, and deer, they kindly traded with me and my men. With sixteen bushels of corn, I returned toward our fort. By the way I encountered with two canoes of Indians from the town and country of Warraskoyack. They requested me to return to their town, where they should load my boat with corn. Thus, with near thirty bushels I returned to our fort.

On the seventeenth of September, Master Wingfield was sent for to the court to answer his slanders against Jehu Robinson and Captain Smith. When president, the gentle Wingfield falsely said that Robinson with others planned to run away with the shallop to Newfoundland, and Robinson now exhibited a complaint against him. My own charge was that he must answer him for that he had said I did conceal an intended mutiny.

Being laid in irons aboard the pinnace had made Wingfield wetter but no less pompous than before. Even after Master Archer had read the complaints, he yet protested.

"Master President," he said, looking down his long nose at Ratliffe, "that which I did was done within the limits of the patent granted us. I therefore pray Master President that I might not be lugged with these disgraces and troubles."

The jury was quick to return its judgement, giving Jehu Robinson one hundred pounds and me two hundred pounds' damages for slander.

"Have you no other eyes and ears than those which grow on Master Recorder's head?" Wingfield complained, glaring at Gabriell Archer.

"If you have wrong, sir," Archer replied, "you might bring your writ of error in London."

At that, Wingfield smiled.

❖·❖·❖·❖

Time thus passing away, our settlement now reasonably fitted with houses, it was concluded that the pinnace and barge should go toward Powhatan to trade for more corn. Lots were cast to decide who should go in her. The chance was mine. While she was fitting, I returned in the barge to Paspihae to trade with that churlish and treacherous nation. After loading but ten or twelve bushels of corn, the salvages there offered to take our swords and pieces by stealth. Failing that, they were ready to assault us, but we remained on guard. When we were coasting the shore, diverse came out of the woods to offer us corn and trade. But, seeing them dog us from place to place, it being night and our necessity not fit for war, we took occasion to return to James Town.

On the ninth of November, with eight men and myself for the barge, we went into the country of Chikhamania for three or four journeys to get provisions for the year following. Three hundred and four hundred bushels were gotten each time, and I unloaded seven or eight hogsheads at our fort. Yet, what I carefully provided, the rest carelessly spent. Wingfield and Kendall, seeing all things at random in my absence, the president's weakness and Martin's never-mending sickness, strengthened themselves with the sailors and other confederates to regain their former credit and authority. Their plan was to take the pinnace, which I had fitted to trade, to alter her course, and go for England.

I might not have known of this plot had it not been for God's grace in touching the heart of Amocis, a salvage, who now came often to the fort and called himself "best friend" to me. He called out to us as we went up the river, gesturing us in to shore.

"Your enemies," he told me, "do take your great ship to England."

Thus it was that I had the plot discovered to me and unexpectedly returned. The pinnace was already set to sail, and much trouble I had to prevent it. I went quickly to the sacre, a thirty-five-hundred-pound piece that shoots a five-and-one-half-pound ball.

I had seen that cannon placed toward the river to defend the fort should a Spanish ship find our town. Jehu Robinson, Thomas Emry, and the laborer George Cassen had been in my company aboard the barge. They were by my side as the sacre was brought to bear upon the pinnace and we fired one shot in warning over the bow.

"Stay, or sink in the river," I called to them on board the pinnace. They stayed.

On the following day, our president had occasion to chide James Read, the blacksmith, for his misdemeanor. In return, the smith not only gave him bad language but also offered to strike him with some of his tools. For this rebellious act, the smith was brought before a jury and condemned to be hanged. Upon being brought to the ladder, Read looked about him, as if hoping for a rescue. Yet none came. The rope was almost about his neck when he saw no other way but death with him.

"Hold," he cried out. "I beg forgiveness, good sirs! Turn me off the ladder and aye, I shall reveal ye a dangerous conspiracy."

Brought down, he was taken into a tent with Ratliffe, Martin, and me. Then, sweating much, the blacksmith confessed that among them was a gentleman who was a spy for the Spanish.

"This gentleman, sirs, ye have held before in chains. He is himself a Catholic, a Papist, sirs. He hath promised gold and safe passage to England for me and, aye, others of our company should we free him, good sirs."

"Tell us his name and we shall spare you," Ratliffe said. The smith's answer came quickly.

"That man, good sirs," Read said, "is Captain Kendall."

It was remembered then that the smith had come aboard the pinnace about some business some three days before. Master Kendall was called before the jury.

Though a base, Papist traitor, Kendall still showed that there was iron in his spine. He stood straight as the charges were read. Before our president could speak his judgement, the condemned man spoke.

"Your Master President," Kendall said, "lacks authority to pronounce judgement. He sayeth his name is Ratliffe. Yet I know that to be false. His real name is Sicklemore. Thus, being false in name and named president under a name not his own, he hath no authority to pronounce judgement."

All eyes turned then to our president, whose face was now the color of sailcloth. We waited for him to deny that accusation, yet he did not. From then on I had little trust in President Captain John Ratliffe Sicklemore, whose reasons for hiding his true name were never discovered.

Martin broke the silence. "None may question my name or authority as member of this council," he said to Kendall. "For your crimes of treason, you shall be shot to death."

And so, within the hour, George Kendall was.

21

POCAHONTAS

The Hunt

All things move in a circle. That is how things were made by Ahone. Just as the Great Sun is a circle and the Moon is a circle, moving with the stars about the sky, so our land is a circle surrounded by the great waters. The days circle and return again and so also do the seasons. Our lives, too, are circles. The time comes to plant and passes by and returns again. The season comes to hunt and passes by and returns again. It was made that way by Ahone, who saw that it was good.

COHONK
TIME OF GEESE FLYING
EARLY DECEMBER 1607

IT WAS A FINE, cold day with small flakes of snow in the air. I watched those snowflakes dancing. I could see my own special name, the name that only my closest friends and family call me, in the feathery snow as I walked around the edge of my father's village. In some places the snow was as deep as my ankles, but in other, sheltered spots the ground was bare and not even frozen. I had picked up several round stones and was rattling them in my hands as I walked along. The sound they made was something like that made by the horns of a buck deer as he strikes his new antlers against a small tree to rub off the dried skin.

This season is the time for hunting deer. Two days before, the hunters from many villages joined together and left for the hunt. My uncle Opechancanough was chosen to be the leader of the communal hunt. As I walked I remembered my father's face while he watched the hunters. Although he certainly appeared calm to all others, it seemed to me that my father was a little sad as the hunters gathered to do the hunting song, danced in a circle about the village, made their offerings to the stones, and then set out.

I continued thinking about my father as the snowflakes danced. Although he is still strong and tall and no one questions his power, he has gray hairs on his chin. Even a Mamanatowic cannot stop the turning of the circle. Not only does a Great Chief not usually leave his people to go into the forest and hunt, my father knows that he is now too old for hunting. I wonder what will happen when the time comes for him to take that road toward the rising sun. When that day comes, I will no longer be the favorite daughter of the Great Chief. I will lose the special place I now enjoy. The leadership of our people will go to my father's brothers. I will no longer be Amonute, the favored one. I will simply be Pocahontas.

"*Nechaun*, my child, things always change."

I have heard my father say that to me many times. Although he is hard as a stone with others, he can be as gentle as a summer breeze when he speaks to me. He first said those words to me when my mother died. He spoke those same words two seasons ago when the puppy that had been following me around fell into the river and drowned. It seems as if I only hear those words when my eyes are wet with tears.

Like a good daughter, I accepted my father's words then and nodded silently. But if I had spoken, I think I would have said, "Yes, but why can they not change for the better?"

Another change, which I have mentioned before, is that the deer are scarcer than in past years. Almost everyone now blames the Coatmen for this. The Tassantassuk are so hungry that they try to kill every deer they see. I do not mean to say that they are successful at this. They are too blind to be good hunters. Unless one of our people is guiding them, the Coatmen can hardly see a deer in the forest when it is close enough to hit with a stone. But their constant hunting makes the deer wary of all humans and frightens them out of our hunting grounds.

I took one of the stones I had been rattling as I walked and threw it at the trunk of an oak tree. It struck with a satisfying *thunk* and bounced down to vanish into the snow.

Then I noticed two men sitting beside the small fire that is kept burning near the place where the *pawcoransak*, the memory stones, are placed. It was Rawhunt and Amocis. The two had been talking about the deer hunt, but they stopped when I came up to them.

They both smiled to see me. It was the proper thing for them to do. One should always be pleased upon seeing the favorite daughter of the Mamanatowic. However, I know that both of them also like me. I am a very easy person to like.

"The hunt will be good," I said. I have heard my father say those words to the hunters before they set out, so I know they are good words to speak.

"Amonute," Rawhunt said with a nod, "if you say so, then it must be so. It must be so."

His voice was so serious that it made me laugh.

"Is it because of the Coatmen that the deer are harder to find now?" I asked, sitting down in front of them. "Have they killed too many deer?"

At that both men laughed, but Rawhunt's face quickly grew serious.

"Amonute," Rawhunt said. "Listen. Those foolish newcomers seem to know nothing, nothing, about how to track a deer or where deer can be found. Our people know where the deer live and how they move back and forth between one place and another in the forest. Thus we go to the place where the deer will be even before the deer get there. But the Coatmen stumble through the woods as if they were blind, making more noise than a wounded bear. Also, those Coatmen do not seem to have any hunting medicine. They have no way of calling the deer to them, as we do. In fact, all that they do has driven the deer away. I think it is not because the deer are afraid of them. I myself think it is because the deer are disgusted with the Tassantassuk."

"That may be so," Amocis said. "That the Coatmen drive away the game animals is one reason why our people are displeased with the Coatmen. The Paspahegh people are the most upset. As you know, those Coatmen placed their camp right in the middle of the Paspahegh hunting grounds, where no wise person would ever think to live. Why would anyone live there in that low, swampy place, where there is not even one single spring with good drinking water? If those Tassantassuk had even as much sense as a little child, they would have moved their camp long ago."

I rattled the rest of the stones in my hands. "Then why have they stayed there?" I asked.

"They are stubborn," Amocis said, smiling in that sly way of his. "I have watched them long enough to see this. They are so stubborn that when they do something wrong they will make ten more mistakes before they admit they are wrong." He held up his hand and began to raise his fingers one by one as he counted off ways the Tassantassuk had shown their stubbornness. *"Necut,"* he said, "they placed their camp in a marshy place but refused to move it even after the little biting ones came in swarms and began to eat them alive. *Ningh,* they still kept casting their nets in the river long after all the fish had gone away. *Nuss,* they continued drinking the water from the river even after the water had become so salty that it made them weak and sick. *Yowgh,* they keep wearing all of their heavy clothing even in the hottest time of the year, when you can see that they were sweating to death. *Paranske,* they have refused to bathe even after they began to smell worse than rotting fish. *Comotinch,* they kept trying to grow crops on land that was no good for growing anything other than marsh grass."

It seemed that Amocis was ready to keep counting until the sun set. Amocis loves to count things.

Rawhunt held up his own hand. "That is enough, my clever friend. That is enough. You may be right. But I have not finished my answer to Amonute about the deer. To be fair, the deer are not just scarce because of the Tassantassuk. I do not know why, but the herds of deer began growing fewer even before the season when three great swan canoes came into view, even before that season."

Rawhunt pointed with his lips at the *pawcoransak,* the carefully piled stones that keep the memory of important things. On one of them, the stone for the hunters, offerings of deer suet and tobacco had been made.

"The stones tell us that this is so. There were great herds of deer in the time of my youth, and hunting them was much easier than today. Now it is not so, not so. For whatever reason, to find enough of them to provide us with skins for clothing and meat to dry for the winter, we must have a communal hunt. With many men and fires, we are able to drive the deer into the circle, where we can kill them."

I rattled my stones again. "So it is as I said, is it not? We *will* have a good hunt. It will be one that our people remember."

Then I carefully selected two of my best stones. I handed the first one, a white stone with small dark lines on it, to Rawhunt. He accepted it from me very carefully and touched it to his forehead. Amocis took the second stone, which was almost completely black, rubbed it between his palms, and then placed it into the pouch that hung from his waist.

We sat together in silence. Then Rawhunt sighed.

"Yes," he said. "Yes, Amonute. I think this hunt will be one that our people will never forget."

22

JOHN SMITH

The River of Chickahominy

The 10th of December, Master Smyth went up the river of the Chechohomynaies to trade for corn. He was desirous to see the head of that river, and when it was not passable with the shallop, he hired a canoe and an Indian to carry him up further. The river the higher grew worse and worse. Then he went on shore with his guide, and left Robinson and Emmery, in the canoe, which were presently slain by the Indians, Pamaonoke's men....

—FROM A DISCOURSE OF VIRGINIA,
BY EDWARD MARIA WINGFIELD

DECEMBER 3RD–6TH, 1607

AFTER THE EXECUTION of Kendall, the traitor, there was much ado for to have the pinnace go for England. Gabriell Archer seemed the main author of this new plan and spent many fine words in setting it forth. No serpent's tongue ever spoke sweeter. Captain Martin and I stood chiefly against it and in fine after many debatings, *pro et contra*, it was resolved to stay a further resolution. I saw that our good recorder, Master Archer, was now even more self-important than had been Wingfield. Alas, his jealousy of my position and reputation grew each day, though I did nothing wrong. Thus it always is that petty men envy their betters and seek to cause their downfall.

Now, with the winter approaching, the rivers became so covered with swans, geese, ducks, and cranes that we daily feasted with good bread, Virginia peas, pumpions and putchamins, fish, fowl, and diverse sorts of wild beasts as fat as we could eat them. So it was that ere long none of our Tuftaffaty humorists, those cranks in fine clothes, desired to go for England.

But our comedies never endured long without a tragedy. Some idle exceptions were muttered against me for not discovering the head of Chickahominy River. It need not to be said which marksman sought to wound me with such arrows of criticism. Taxed by the council to be not slow in so worthy an attempt, on the third of December I set forth in the barge, taking with me eight of our men, to finish this discovery.

It was not an easy passage. It was only with much labor that we proceeded so far by cutting trees in sunder. Then the river became narrower, only eight or ten feet at a high water, the stream exceeding swift and the bottom hard channel. Rather than to endanger the barge by going further upstream to seek a lake that might rise there, we resolved to hire a canoe. We then returned the barge to Apocant, where there was a broad bay. There we anchored in the middle of the bay, well out of danger of shot.

On my earlier voyage up this river, certain Indians had hailed us with the cry of *"wingapo,"* placing their hands upon their breasts in proof of friendship. One of them, known as Nauiraus, had conducted us before on another voyage and learned to speak well our language. He often had offered to conduct me about his country, for his people were eager to trade with us. So it was that he and a friend joined us with their canoe early on this present voyage. They assured me that they could now guide me up the river and that all would be well.

I chose two men who had proven themselves somewhat in the past, Jehu Robinson and Thomas Emry, to go with me in the canoe of the naturals.

"Listen well," I then said to the six men left in the barge. "Mark my words. None are to go ashore until my return."

Some wise men may now accuse me of too much in indiscretion. Yet they might have done the same if they well consider the proven friendship of the Indians in accompanying us and the seeming desolateness of the country around us, a vast and wild wilderness. Nor could they have predicted the foolishness of the men left in the barge. Alas, I was not long absent before my men ignored those last orders and went ashore.

Their want of government gave both occasion and opportunity to the salvages who had concealed themselves along the river. They surprised one George Cassen, who decided to wade to the shore. He had scarce set foot on the sand before he was taken and bound to a tree. Ere long the unfortunate Cassen had been forced to tell them that his Captain, John Smith, had taken a canoe up the river and into the marshes to hunt fowls. Whereupon the salvages slew Cassen and set the tree to which he was tied afire.

The five remaining men aboard the barge narrowly escaped being cut off by the Indians. They hied back to James Town like rabbits fleeing the fox, bearing word that John Smith had surely been taken, tortured, and killed.

Little dreaming of that accident, I had by now been led by my Indian guide twenty miles further into the desert. There my two men and I went ashore to refresh ourselves and make a fire to boil our victuals. Seeing it would be some time before our food was cooked, I decided to see the nature of the soil about us. Nauiraus was eager to show me about.

"Many fat fowl to shoot in marsh," he told me.

The other Indian, having made a good fire, now said that he would walk along the river to gather more wood. Declaring themselves weary from our long journey, Master Robinson and Emry chose to wait by the warmth of the fire.

It seemed that there was nothing to fear. Yet, long years of war had taught me to be ever at the ready. Alas that my men, one a gentleman and the other trained only to be a carpenter, did not share that readiness.

"Master Robinson," I said, bearing in mind that, with his higher station, Robinson should be in charge while I was away, "will you keep watch whilst I take a short walk to spy the land about?"

"I shall," Robinson said.

"And I as well," Thomas Emry chimed in. I looked the two of them up and down, not knowing it would be the last sight I would ever have of them living. They had not the look of soldiers, and I bethought it wise to advise them how they should behave.

"Keep your matches lit," I said. "You need be in order to discharge a piece for my retreat at the sight of any Indians."

But within a quarter of an hour, I heard not a warning shot but a loud cry and a hollowing of Indians.

23

Trouble

Long ago, Arakun's face was not blackened. But Arakun was the same then as he is now, always wanting to touch everything with his hands and always, always walking around everywhere and looking for trouble. One of the things he loved to do was to tease people and frighten them. So he would creep up on people at night and leap out at them to make them scream with fright.

One night Arakun came creeping out of the forest and saw an old woman sitting alone by a small fire outside her yihacan.

"Waugh," Arakun said. "This is good. I will frighten her."

Then he crept close to her, but the old woman had seen him coming. When Arakun jumped up and made a great noise, that old woman threw a handful of hot ashes into his face. Arakun ran off and leaped into the river to wash off his face. To this day Arakun is always washing his hands and face in the river. But where those hot ashes struck him, his fur was blackened and it remains so to this day. People see the blackened face of Arakun and they say to their children, "You see what happens when you go looking for trouble?"

NEWS ABOUT THE Coatmen has arrived at our village. It is said that everyone and everything, sooner or later, must come to the village of the Mamanatowic. Some people come here because it is the turn of their village to bring the share of deerskins or corn that belongs to him. Some come because the greatest of the *quiyoughsokuk* are here by my father's side and their advice is often sought. Some come because they are *werowansuk* in league with my father and they must make plans together or gain his approval for their actions.

Many also come because of the dancing and singing that takes place here at the times of the special festivals and ceremonies that come with every new season. It is the singing and dancing that I love the best. I am one of the best singers of all the young women. That is why I am always the one to lead the young women's dances, even though I have heard some jealous people whisper that I am only asked to do this because I am my father's favorite. Jealousy can make it hard for people to see the truth, especially when those who are jealous are not good at doing something.

Some people come to Werowocomoco because they wish to come here. Some come here even if it is against their wishes. So it is with those who have done wrong and are brought to be punished. So it is with the *werowansuk* and their families of those villages and those who seek to defy my father's alliance or try to go to war against him. After their warriors are defeated, those highborn ones are brought here. It does not make them happy. Of course, they are not tortured or killed. Who would ever dream of doing that to a werowance and who could be so bad hearted as to hurt women and children? But being here under the control of my father is bitter to them. It reminds them of their defeat. It reminds them that their power is much less than the power of the Mamanatowic and his alliance of many nations.

I have sometimes wondered what it would be like for me to be taken into captivity. I know that I would be treated well. This is not just because I am the daughter of Powhatan. I am a very likable person. But I do not think I would enjoy being a captive. What I would like least of all would be not knowing all that is happening. Captives are never told much of anything.

Because everyone comes to Werowocomoco, news of everything that happens comes here as well. It is of no use to try to keep that news secret. Even the power of a Mamanatowic cannot stop the people from talking. That is especially true when the news is of some great deed done in battle. Our warriors are proud of their courage and will gladly brag to anyone of the great things they have done—or make up a song about it. That kind of bravery makes my father glad. He knows that his power comes from the bravery of the men and the good minds of the women of our nations. No one could remain in such a high place as he holds were the women and men not behind him. Though it is said that my father is feared, it is also true that he is respected. Without respect, no one can ask the people to do anything.

It is also known that the great power of Okeus, the god who watches over the doings of the people, is behind my father. I am not always sure that I like what Okeus says. Okeus seems to like fighting. But Ahone, the great peaceful one who made all things, does not speak directly to the people as Okeus does. Ahone does not place his spirit into an image that the priests can speak with. If he did, I know that I would listen to it. I wonder what Ahone would say about what we should do with the Coatmen.

The latest news is that a fight has taken place with some of the Tassantassuk who stumbled into the midst of our great hunt. They had no reason to be there, and it angered our men to see them poking their noses in. Some thought that they had come as a raiding party, ready to do battle with our people, but when they were caught, most of those Coatmen did not behave well at all. They did not even show as much bravery as a boy who has not yet been reborn.

I have decided to ask Rawhunt more about it. As my father's adviser, he always knows the best truth of such events. It is early morning and I have already gone down to the water, broken the thin ice to wash myself, and spoken my morning thanks to Kefgawes, whose light made the water glitter like *rawrenock* beads. Rawhunt smiles when he sees me coming up from the river. He is sitting in front of his *yihacan*, but he is not alone. My brother Naukaquawis is with him, and he, too, smiles as he turns to look at me. It is as if they already know what I am about to ask. Although the snow was on the ground, it is a warm day. So Naukaquawis is enjoying the sun on his bare chest and shoulders.

"Amonute," Rawhunt says, squinting at me, "what, what could it be that you want to know?"

I sit down in the snow next to my brother and wrap my arms around my legs.

"Why are the Coatmen always traveling about and looking at things?" I ask. "What is it they are looking for?"

"Ah, ah, ah," Rawhunt says, shaking his head. "Even among our own people, it is hard to say what is within another man's heart unless that person chooses to tell you. It is even harder, even harder, when it comes to the Tassantassuk. For although they have often told us what they are doing, it still makes no sense, no sense. They say they are going up and down our rivers because they are looking for stones to make ax heads. Yet we know their own axes are better than ours, which are made of stone. They say they are seeking the way to get to an enemy people who harmed one of their people in the past, yet they spend their time making the walls of their camp stronger, as if they wish to stay right where they are, right where they are. They say that their largest swan canoe has only sailed away to Kecoughtan and will return soon with its great thunder weapons. Yet we know that it sailed far out into the great salt waters two whole seasons ago. They say that they want to be our friends, and then they beat our people and treat us like dogs when we visit them. I am afraid that it is as hard for the Coatmen to speak the truth as it is for most of them to show real courage, real courage."

Rawhunt pauses and pokes at the ground before him with a stick, making a shape in the snow like that of a crawling snake. "It also seems that even though most of them lack courage, for some reason those Coatmen are always looking, looking for trouble."

"What happened in the fight?" I ask.

Naukaquawis snorts. "Fight? It was hardly that, my sister. Some of the men of Paspahegh took one of the Coatmen prisoner when he came wading onto the shore from their big *quintans*. As soon as the others on their boat saw us, they took their *quintans* down the river to escape, leaving their friend behind." Naukaquawis scoops up a handful of snow and tosses it to one side. "*Matah!* It is bad that they were such cowards. The Paspahegh men recognized the Coatman they had captured as one who had treated them like dogs, hitting them and pushing them down when they visited the Coatmen's fort. But now that he was caught, he began to cry out and weep like a baby. They gave him every chance to show his courage as a warrior. If he had done so, they might have spared his life. But all he did was scream and cry for mercy. He even pointed out to them the way that the *quintans* carrying three other Coatmen from his party had gone. That he showed such cowardice embarrassed the men of Paspahegh greatly."

My brother shakes his head and looks over at Rawhunt.

Rawhunt stabs at the shape he has made in the snow with his stick. Then he takes up the story where my brother had left off.

"As to the others," Rawhunt says, "the other three who went up into the marsh with the *quintans*, your uncle Opechancanough and his Pamaunkees found two of them. They were asleep by a fire, asleep! When the two Tassantassuk woke and saw they were surrounded, they were so frightened that they did not even try to use their thunder weapons. Instead, they tried to run, to run. Your uncle's warriors were so disgusted that they did not even try to take those cowards prisoner. They just shot them with arrows and left them there, left them there."

Rawhunt stops talking and looks down at the snow. It does not make him happy to think of how badly those Coatmen had died. If your enemies do not show real courage, it weakens your own heart. I feel bad, too. Why do the Coatmen have to fight us this way? Why can they not try to live with us in peace, respect us, and behave as honest friends? Then I remember something Rawhunt said. There were three Coatmen in the *quintans*.

"Rawhunt," I say, "wait. What happened to the third man?"

Rawhunt lifts his head, and I see the twinkle in his eyes. My brother looks over at him and chuckles. They have been teasing me, testing me to see if I have been listening carefully, by not telling me the whole story.

"Ah," Rawhunt says. "This is where the story becomes interesting, becomes interesting. That third man was their werowance, Little Red-Haired Warrior himself."

"Unh-hunh," my brother adds, smiling broadly. "Unlike the others, he knew how to fight!"

24

JOHN SMITH

Captured

This wyroans Pamaunche I hold to inhabit a rich land of copper and pearl. His country lies into the land of another river, which by relation and description of the savages comes also from the mountains Quirank, but a shorter journey. The copper he had, as also many of his people, was very flexible. I bowed a piece of the thickness of a shilling round my finger as if it had been lead. I found them nice in parting with any. They wear it in their ears, about their necks in long links, and in broad plates on their heads. So we made no great unquiry of it, neither seemed desirous to have it.

The king had a chain of pearl about his neck thrice double, the third part of them as big as peas, which I could not value less worth than 3 of 400li, had the pearl been taken from the muskle as it ought to be.

His kingdom is full of deer; so also is most of all the kingdoms.

He hath as the rest likewise many rich furs.

This place I call "Pamaunche's Palace," howbeit by Nauviraus his words the King of Winauk is possessor herof. The plat of ground is bare without wood some 100 acres,

where are set beans, wheat, peas, tobacco, gourds, pompions,
and other things unknown to us in our tongue.

—FROM A RELATION OF THE DISCOVERY OF OUR RIVER
FROM JAMES FORT INTO THE MAIN, MADE BY CAPTAIN
CHRISTOFER NEWPORT, AND SINCERELY WRITTEN AND
OBSERVED BY A GENTLEMAN OF THE COLONY

DECEMBER 6TH–30TH, 1607

UPON HEARING THAT loud cry, I supposed that my guide, Nauiraus, had betrayed me. Presently I seized him and bound his arm to mine with my garters, my pistol ready bent to be avenged upon him. Yet he seemed innocent of what was done.

"Fly," Nauiraus said. "Must take flight."

Flight was not an easy thing, for I stood at the edge of a quagmire and the sound of shouting had come from the one path that had led us to this place. So I told my guide, asking how we might otherwise take flight.

But as we went on discoursing, I was struck by an arrow on my right thigh. It did me little harm and I turned to espy two Indians drawing their bows, which I prevented in discharging a French pistol. By the time I had charged again, three or four more Indians had done the like, taking the place of the first who had fallen down and fled. At my next discharge, they also fell and fled. Now my guide I made my barricado, who offered not to strive but allowed me to use him as my buckler. The aim of the salvages was such that not a single arrow struck him, and his bulk was so much greater than mine that he made a fine shield. Twenty or thirty arrows were shot against me, but fell short or stuck in my clothes with no great hurt.

Three or four more times I discharged his pistol ere the

King of Pamaunkee, called Opechancanough, with two hundred men environed me. At his command, each drew their bows and then laid them upon the ground without shot. My guide then treated betwixt them and me conditions of peace.

"This man," Nauiraus said, reaching back to touch my arm and then gesturing upward with his palm, "he werowance, Captain."

At that the King nodded and spoke words, much of which I could not understand.

"King say Coatmen all slain, give him your weapon," Nauiraus explained.

At that I smiled. "Tell him I shall not fire again. I shall go to my boat."

I then began to retire. Minding the salvages more than I did my steps, I stepped fast into the quagmire. Nauiraus, in trying to pull me forth, also did the same, and the two of us began to sink deeper.

Thus surprised, I resolved to try their mercies. My arms I cast from me, till which none had dared approach him.

Having thrown away my arms, the salvages accepted my surrender. They drew me forth from the oozy creek and led me to the fire, where Jehu Robinson lay slain with twenty or thirty arrows in him. Emry I saw not.

Diligently they chafed my benumbed limbs. I demanded they take me to their Captain, who had retired to his pavilion. So they showed me to Opechancanough, King of Pamaunkee. To him I gave a round ivory double compass dial. Much he marveled at the playing of the fly and needle which he could see so plainly and yet not touch because of the glass that covered them. When I demonstrated by that globe-like jewel the roundness of the earth and skies, the sphere of the sun, moon, and stars and how the sun does chase the night round the world continually, and many other like such matters, they all stood as amazed with admiration.

Notwithstanding, within an hour after that, they tied me to a tree, and as many as could stand about prepared to shoot me, but the King held up the compass in his hand. They all laid down their bows and arrows and in a triumphant manner led me to Orapaks, where I was after their manner kindly feasted and well used.

Their manner in conducting me was thus: drawing themselves all in file, the King in the middest had all their pieces and swords borne before him. I was led after him by three great salvages holding me fast by each arm and on each side six more went in file with their arrows nocked. But upon our arriving at the town (which was only thirty or forty hunting houses made of mats, which they remove as they please, as we our tents), with all the women and children staring to behold me, the soldiers then cast themselves into a ring, dancing in such several postures and singing and yelling out such hellish notes and screeches. All were strangely painted, and every one had his quiver of arrows and at his back a club, on his arm a fox or otter skin. Every man had his head and shoulders painted red with oil and puccoon mingled together, which scarlet-like color made an exceeding handsome show. Each had his bow in his hand and the skin of a bird, with her wings abroad dried, tied upon his head, or a piece of copper, a white shell, a long feather with a small rattle at the tails of their snakes tied to it, or some such like toy.

All this time I and the King stood in the middest guarded, as before it was said, and after three dances the King and his men departed. The others conducted me to a long house, where thirty or forty tall fellows did guard me. Ere long more bread and venison was brought me than would serve twenty men. I think my stomach at that time was not very good. What I left, my keepers put into baskets. About midnight they set the meat before me again. All this time not one of them would eat a bit with me, till the next morning they brought me as much and more and then did eat the old and reserved me the new. It made me think they would fat me to eat me.

Yet even as I was in this desperate estate, one Maocassater—whom I had met before—came into the long house and gave me his gown to defend me from the cold. This was, I suppose, in requital of some beads and toys I had given him at my first arrival in Virginia.

25

POCAHONTAS

Waiting

Long ago, the people forgot to greet Kefgawes, the Sun. Instead of looking up to Sun and giving thanks, they complained that Sun hurt their eyes. So, one day, Sun decided to no longer look down upon our land. The day of the Moon ended, but Sun stayed beyond the edge of the world.

When the people woke that morning, there was no light. They became afraid in the darkness, and cried for help. Great Hare heard their cries. He went to Sun and begged him to return.

"The people do not welcome me," Sun said. "I will stay here."

Great Hare turned to the Spider for help. "Make a net for me," he said, and Spider did so. Great Hare threw that spiderweb net over Sun and pulled him back across the sky. As soon as Sun became visible to our people, they began to cry out words of welcome.

Hearing those words, Sun changed his mind. "The people are glad to see me," he said. "As long as they remember to give me thanks each morning, I shall always return."

Great Hare pulled the spiderweb net off the Sun. Some strands, though, remained. We see them when Sun shines through clouds. And as long as the people give thanks each dawn, Sun will bring them light.

I USUALLY AM ABLE to sleep throughout the night. Even the regular calls made by the guards who walk around my father's great *yihacan* do not wake me. But this night has been different. I hear the soft sounds of those four men who stand alert all through the night outside the big longhouse, one at each corner post. They are not allowed to sleep. So they shuffle their feet, and now and then thump the ground with their spears. Twelve times every night they must sound the call to prove that all is well and safe in each of the four directions.

"*Ya-hoo,*" calls the man who stands at the post in the direction of the dawn.

"*Ya-hoo,*" answers the man at the corner post in the Summer Land direction.

"*Ya-hoo,*" now comes from the direction of the sunset.

"*Ya-hoo,*" the Winter Land guard replies.

Then, their circuit completed, they wait again in silence. Should any of them fail to answer the call, it might mean that an enemy had silenced him, and a general alarm would be sounded. Then forty men, the tallest of all the warriors in our villages, who always sleep close by to guard the Mamanatowic, come running with their torches, weapons ready. If they find that the silence of a sentry is simply because he has fallen asleep, that man is then beaten to punish him. It has been a long time since any sentry has fallen asleep at his post, and no enemies have ever attacked our village in the night.

Yet my father does not relax his guard. It is another of the weights he always carries as the Great Chief. I asked him once why we must always be on guard when no one ever dares to attack us.

"My favorite daughter," he said, his face almost smiling, "it is because we are always on guard that we are safe." Then he looked toward the sunrise direction, and the heaviness of sorrow came back into his eyes. "It may not always be this way."

That circle of calls about my father's great *yihacan* has now been sounded ten times. Soon it will be time to go down to the water and give my morning thanks and greeting to the Sun. And I have not slept at all. I am waiting, as is everyone else in Werowocomoco. I hope that my lack of sleep does not make my face puffy or my eyes red. It is important that I look my best today.

With the dawn my uncle Opechancanough will bring the Coatman captive. The one they caught is no other than my Little Red-Haired Warrior, the only Coatman who knows how to fight. He is so different from all the others that he is more like a real person, like one of us, than a Tassantassak. My father has hopes for him.

I think of the stories that have come to us in the last twenty-five days since Little Red-Haired Warrior was first taken prisoner in a big fight. His men were as easy to defeat as foolish rabbits, but he acted like a warrior. Even though he was surrounded by two hundred men, he refused to surrender. Only the swamp was able to overcome him, sucking him into it until he had to give up his weapon or be swallowed by the mud. I laughed when I was told about how the earth itself defeated Little Red-Haired Warrior.

Part of it was the story and part of my laughter came from the way Rawhunt acted out the part of Little Red-Haired Warrior, stepping back into the mud and then, with a look of displeasure on his face, sinking deeper and deeper.

Strong as the weapons of the Coatmen may be, our land is stronger. It, too, fights on our side. We have seen how the numbers of the Coatmen at their walled village keep growing smaller. A few of them have been killed by our arrows, but more of them have been killed by the river or their own stupidity.

After Little Red-Haired Warrior was caught, Opechancanough took him to the big hunting camp at Rasawrack. He made sure that the Coatman was treated as a werowance should be treated. This was not easy, for Little Red-Haired Warrior had killed two men and injured others. There were many who wanted to tie him to a tree and fill him with arrows until he looked like a porcupine. Through it all, Little Red-Haired Warrior behaved well. Now that he was not fighting us, he no longer acted angry. He did not weep or scream or plead for his life as other Coatmen had done when captured.

My uncle admired the way Little Red-Haired Warrior showed no fear. Also, as proof of his friendly intentions, he sat down and showed my uncle some of his medicine objects. One of them was a circle of metal with a round piece of ice in it that never melted. Under that ice was a stick that spun about. With signs and the few words of our language he spoke, Little Red-Haired Warrior explained to my uncle how he, too, gave respect to the Sun and the Great Circle of life.

My uncle was pleased, but to make certain that he could trust the Coatman warrior, he called the *quiyoughsokuk* and asked them to consult with Okeus and the other spirits that listen.

With great care, the priests made their circles of cornmeal about the fire. They laid down the sacred kernels of corn and the sticks that would speak to them with the voices of Okeus and the helpful spirits. They sang the powerful songs and listened to the voices that answered. Finally, after three days, they told my uncle that Little Red-Haired Warrior meant our people no harm. This pleased my uncle even more.

Little Red-Haired Warrior then gave my uncle a gift. It was a bag filled with the black grains that burn and make the weapons of the Coatmen thunder. It is my uncle's plan to plant the black grains in the spring as we do our corn. Our earth is so fertile that surely we will grow a great crop of those black grains.

My uncle then took Little Red-Haired Warrior to his town of Paspahegh and to other towns of our people, showing him our strength and how good our lives are.

At Rappahannock, the werowance came to look at Little Red-Haired Warrior to see if he was the captain of the Coatmen who had come there four turnings of the leaves ago. That captain was the one who behaved so badly and killed the previous werowance. But as soon as the werowance of Rappahannock stood close to Little Red-Haired Warrior, he saw that he was not the man. He touched the top of his own head and then lowered his hand to his chest.

"*Waugh,*" the werowance of Rappahannock laughed. "This Coatman is only half the size of that one. Welcome, *nettoppew!*"

It is the hope of both my uncle and my wise father that Little Red-Haired Warrior now understands how much better it is to live as we live. Perhaps today, after meeting my father, he will decide to join us. He will get us thunder weapons that we can use to defend ourselves. He will help us get rid of those other rude and worthless Tassantassuk.

My father has told me that I will also have a special part to play. I have thought about it all night. I am more than ready for the dawn.

26

JOHN SMITH

The Great King

The inhabitants themselves, especially his frontier neighbor princes, call him still Powhatan; his own people sometimes call him Ottaniack, sometimes Mananatowick, which last signifies "great king"; but his proper right name which they salute him with is Wahunsenacawh; the greatness and bounds of whose empire by reason of his powerfulness and ambition in his youth hath larger limits than ever had any of his predecessors in former times. . . .

He is a goodly old man, not shrinking though well beaten with many cold and stormy winters, in which he hath been patient of many necessities and attempts of his fortune to make his name and family great. He is supposed to be little less than 80 years old (I dare not say how much more others say he is); of a tall stature and clean limbs, of a sad aspect, round fat visaged, with gray hairs, some hairs upon his chin and so on his upper lip.

—FROM THE HISTORY OF TRAVEL
BY WILLIAM STRACHEY

TWO DAYS AFTER, a man would have slain me but that the guards prevented it. That man sought revenge for the death of his son whom I had wounded, to whom they conducted me and asked me to recover the poor man then breathing his last. I told them that at James Town I had a water would do it if they would let me go to fetch it, but they would not permit that.

Craving my advice, the salvages then told me of the preparations they had made to assault James Town. They were solicited to do so by the King of Paspihae. They promised me that for recompense I should have life, liberty, land, and women.

"There is great difficulty and danger," I said to the salvages.

I told them of the mines, the great guns and other engines, which exceedingly affrighted them. Ere long their cruel minds towards the fort I had diverted in describing the ordnance and mines in the field as well as the revenge Captain Newport would take of them at his return.

I then told the King that I desired to have a messenger sent to James Town with a letter I would write, by which they should understand how kindly they had used me, and that I was well, lest they should revenge my death.

King Opechancanough granted this. In part of a table book I wrote my mind to them at the fort, telling them what was intended, how they should follow my directions to afright the messengers, and without fail send me such things as I writ for in an inventory I sent with them. According to my request, the salvages went to James Town, in as bitter weather as could be of frost and snow. Within three days they returned and told of how when they came to James Town, seeing men sally out as I had told them they would, they left my table book and fled. Yet in the night they came again to the place where I had told them they should receive an answer. There they found such things as I had promised them. This was told to the wonder of all them that heard it, who concluded that I could either divine the future or that the paper could speak.

They then led me to the Youghtaunends, the Mattapanients, the Paiankatanks, the Nantaughtacunds, and Onawmanients upon the rivers of Rappahannock and Potowameck, over all those rivers and back again by diverse other several nations, to the King's habitation at Pamaunkee, where they entertained me with most strange and fearful conjurations,

> As if neare led to hell,
> Amongst the Devils to dwell.

So would the poet Lucretius have it. Not long after, early in the morning a great fire was made in a long house and a mat spread on the one side. They caused me to sit and all the guards went out of the house. Presently came skipping a great grim fellow with a hellish voice and a rattle in his hand. He was all painted over with coal mingled with oil, and he wore many snakes' and weasels' skins stuffed with moss, all their tails tied together so they met on the crown of his head in a tassel. Round about the tassel was a coronet of feathers, the skins hanging round about his head, back, and shoulders.

With most strange gestures and passions he began his invocation, and environed the fire with a circle of meal. Which done, three more like such devils came rushing in with the like antic tricks, painted half-black, half-red, but all their eyes were painted white and they wore some red strokes like mustaches along their cheeks. Round about me these fiends danced a pretty while, and then in came three more as ugly as the rest, with red eyes and white strokes down their black faces.

At last they all sat down right against me, three of them on the one hand of the chief Priest, and three on the other. Then, with all their rattles, they began a song, which when it ended, the chief Priest laid down five wheat corns. Then, straining his arms and hands with such violence that he sweat and his veins swelled, he began a short oration. At the conclusion they all gave a short groan and then laid down three grains more. After that began their song again and then another oration, ever laying down so many corns as before until they had twice encircled the fire. At the end of every song or oration, they laid down a stick between the divisions of corn.

Till six o'clock in the evening neither I nor they did eat or drink, and then they feasted merrily with the best provision they could make. Three days they used this ceremony, the meaning whereof, they told me, was to know if I intended them well or no. The circle of meal signified their country, the circle of corn the bounds of the sea, and the sticks my country. They imagined the world to be round and flat like a trencher, and they in the middest. After this they brought in my bag of gunpowder, which they carefully preserved till the next spring to plant as they did their corn because they would be acquainted with the nature of that seed. Opitchapam, the Great King's brother, invited me to his house where, with many platters of bread, fowl, and wild beasts he bid me welcome, but not any of them would eat a bit with me, but put the remainder in baskets. At my return to Opechancanough's, all the King's women and their children flocked round me for their parts, as due by custom, to be merry with such fragments.

At last they brought me to Meronocomoco, where was

Powhatan, their Emperor. More than two hundred of those grim courtiers stood wondering at me, as if I had been a monster, till Powhatan and his train had put themselves in their greatest braveries. Before a fire upon a seat like a bedstead, a foot high upon ten or twelve mats, their Emperor proudly sat. He was richly hung with a great many chains of great pearl about his neck and covered with a great robe made of rarowcun skins, and all the tails hanging by. At his head sat a woman, at his feet another. On each side, sitting upon the ground, were ranged his chief men, ten in a rank, and behind them as many women, with all their heads and shoulders painted red, many of their heads bedecked with the white down of birds and each with a great chain of white beads about her neck.

At my entrance before the Great King, all the people gave a great shout. The Emperor had such a grave and majestical countenance as drove me into admiration to see such a state in a naked salvage. He kindly welcomed me with good words. Opossunoquonuske, the Queen of Appamattuck, was appointed to bring me water, and another brought me a bunch of feathers, in stead of a towel to dry my hands. Having feasted me after their best barbarous manner they could, a long consultation was held.

The Emperor asked me the cause of our coming.

"We had been in a fight with the Spaniards, our enemies," I told him. "Being overpowered, near put to retreat and troubled by extreme weather, we put to this shore where, landing at Chesepiock, the people shot at us, but at Kecoughtan they kindly used us. We by signs demanded fresh water. They described us up the river was all fresh. At Paspihae also they kindly used us. Our pinnace being leaky, we were inforced to stay to mend her till Captain Newport, my father, came to conduct us away."

He demanded why we went further with our boat.

On the other side of their land, I told him, where was salt water, my father had a child slain. His death we intended to revenge. It was, we supposed, the Monacans, his enemies, who had done this.

It seemed he accepted my lies as truth. After good deliberation, he began to describe to me the countries beyond the falls, confirming what not only Opechancanough but also an Indian who had been prisoner to Powhatan before had told me. Some called it five days, some six, some eight where the said water dashed among stones and rocks.

Atquanachuke he described to be the people that had slain my brother, whose death he would revenge. Many kingdoms he described to the head of the bay. I requited his discourse, seeing what pride he had in his great and spacious domains, seeing that all he knew were under his territories.

I then described to him the territories of Europe, which was subject to our great King, and the innumerable multitude of his ships. I gave him to understand the noise of trumpets and the terrible manner of fighting under Captain Newport, his father, who was the werowance of all the waters. At his greatness Powhatan admired and not a little feared.

But the conclusion was that two great stones were brought before Powhatan. He spoke stern words to me, like unto those of a death sentence. Then as many salvages as could laid hands upon me, dragged me to the stones, and thereon laid my head, ready with their clubs to beat out my brains.

27

POCAHONTAS

The Promise

One of the greatest gifts given us by Ahone is tobacco. Its smoke carries our words when we pray. The great Road of Stars in the sky is white from the smoke that has risen with the prayers of our people.

When we travel upon the rivers or into the Great Salt Water Bay, we carry tobacco with us. If the wind should rise and the waters grow rough, we take that tobacco and offer it to the wind and water. Then, accepting our gift, hearing the truth of our words, the wind grows quiet and the waters grow calm.

So it is that when we have a great ceremony, when we gather to speak in council, we place tobacco into the central fire. Then the words that we speak are true, and our promises are sacred.

COHONK
TIME OF LONG NIGHTS
LATE DECEMBER 1607

MY BROTHER AND I watch as my father welcomes Little Red-Haired Warrior. It is good to hear the words that my father speaks to him. He explains our ways, how he has brought together the many villages and nations in a great alliance. Together they are strong. Now, if Little Red-Haired Warrior will help us, if he will bring us some of his powerful weapons, then no one could defeat us.

It seems that Little Red-Haired Warrior is listening well. When he speaks, making gestures with his hands and using those few words of ours that he knew, it seems clear that he recognizes my father's greatness. He asks for his help and shows himself ready to become one with us. The Monacan people have killed one of Little Red-Haired Warrior's brothers. So he has been going up and down our rivers, trying to find his way to the land of those people who are our enemies, too. He wants to seek revenge.

My father stands.

"As Mamanatowic," he says, "the power of life is mine. I am the one who will revenge the death of your brother."

He gestures to his guards. They take Little Red-Haired Warrior by his arms and lead him to the stones of justice. They press him down upon the stones and turn his head so that he can see them up close.

"On these stones," my father says, his voice deep and stern, "those who have done great wrong are executed."

From the shadowed side of the longhouse, where I stand with Naukaquawis, I can see how moved Little Red-Haired Warrior is by my father's words. He stares at those stones and bites down on his lip.

"Now," my father continues, "your revenge will be my revenge. You have died as Tassantassuk. You have been reborn as a member of my own family."

He points with his lips toward the place where my brother and I stand in the shadows. Until now, Little Red-Haired Warrior has not seen us. My brother walks out slowly, with the dignity befitting a son of the Mamanatowic. But we have been waiting a long time, and I cannot help myself. I leave my brother behind and run right up to Little Red-Haired Warrior. His eyes widen as he sees me. I am sure he is impressed with how fine I look adorned with my paint and the glitter of *matchqueon* all over my head and shoulders and bare chest and my best apron, with its embroidery of *rawrenock*. I kneel and throw my arms around his neck.

"You are my older brother," I say to him. "I will always be your child."

The men who held him close to the stones of justice raise Little Red-Haired Warrior to his feet. I take hold of his arm, noticing that my brother—who has not been as quick as I was to claim our new uncle—has done the same on the other side. My brother looks over at me and shakes his head. I stick out my tongue at him. I have gotten to our new uncle first, and so I will always be the first of his relatives among our people.

My father clears his throat, and we turn to look at him.

"Now it is done," my father says. "Now you will always be our friend and our relative. You will leave Paspahegh and come to live close to us. You will now be werowance of Capahowsick. I will give you venison and corn and whatever you need to eat. You will send me two great thunder weapons and a grindstone."

My father pauses as he looks first at my brother and then at me. "Cabden Jonsammit, Little Red-Haired Warrior. You shall be as dear to me as my son Naukaquawis. You shall make bells and beads and copper for my daughter Pocahontas. It shall be that way."

He reaches out his hand and Rawhunt holds forth a tobacco pouch. My father takes out a great handful of tobacco. He holds it up to the sky, to the four winds, to the earth, and then tosses it into the fire. His promises are sacred now. As long as Little Red-Haired Warrior and his people live by those words, they will be our friends.

I am happy this day, as I stand there and I squeeze the hand of my new brother. Little Red-Haired Warrior looks down at me and then, gently, squeezes my hand back. His grim face changes as, for the first time, he smiles. My heart becomes so full that it feels like the river when it overflows as the tide rises.

We shall live together in peace, I think. *We shall live together in peace.*

Afterword

In some ways, things turned out as Pocahontas had hoped. A period of relative peace followed the incident at Werowocomoco. Pocahontas became a regular visitor to Jamestown and a favorite of many of the first colonists, especially John Smith.

It is likely that Powhatan believed that John Smith had become, like one of his subject werowances, a true ally who would be loyal to the Mamanatowic. However, that was not so. Smith's agenda was more ambitious. Even if he was a white man with a better understanding of the Indians than most, it seems clear he never really saw things through Indian eyes. During the remaining twenty-one months of Smith's stay in Virginia, relations between Jamestown and the Powhatan nations were sometimes good and sometimes at the brink of war. Through it all Pocahontas appears to have remained an influential voice for peace.

Ironically, Smith's fellow colonists were as much a danger to him as the Indians were. On his return to Jamestown, after being taken captive and released by Powhatan, Captain Smith was arrested and charged with causing the deaths of the men who were killed on that ill-fated expedition up the river. Once again, he managed to win acquittal and escape execution, but the infighting of the Jamestown colonists was far from over, even though Smith eventually became president of the quarreling, often lazy settlers.

What might have happened had Captain John Smith remained in Virginia will never be known. In September 1609, in what may have been an accident or a deliberate act on the part of someone who wished to harm him, Smith was terribly injured. While returning to Jamestown in a canoe, he fell asleep and the bag of gunpowder on his waist was somehow ignited. Then, as Smith records in *The Proceedings of the English Colony in Virginia,* while he lay in bed recuperating from serious burns, an assassin made an overt attempt to kill him with a "mercilesse Pistoll." Even when wounded, Smith was formidable enough to frighten off the would-be killer, whose "hart did fail him." On October 4, 1609, realizing that the odds were against him, Captain John Smith set sail for England, never to return to Virginia.

Pocahontas, who appears to have cared for John Smith as one loves a favorite uncle, was told that Captain Smith had died. It seems certain that she grieved his death, for when she finally encountered him again in England years later, she felt so shocked (and perhaps betrayed) that at first she could not speak to him.

Pocahontas's story did not end with Smith's departure. She eventually became the catalyst for the longest period of amity between the English and the Powhatan nations. That period, 1614 to 1622, has been called the Peace of Pocahontas. She converted to Christianity in 1614, married the English colonist John Rolfe, and gave birth to a son, Thomas, in 1615. In 1616, the little family sailed to England. Their mission was to gain support for the Virginia Colony, including a school for Powhatan children. As they were preparing to sail back to Virginia, Pocahontas, who had been ill, became very sick. At

Gravesend, England, within sight of the sea that divided her from her homeland, she breathed her last. Her final words to her husband, recorded in a letter written in 1617 by John Rolfe to Sir Edwin Sandys, were "All must die. 'Tis enough that the child liveth."

Early Seventeenth-Century English

The English spoken and written by John Smith and the other colonists was the same English used by William Shakespeare. (In fact, one of Shakespeare's plays, *The Tempest*, was drawn from a Virginia colonist's account of being shipwrecked in Bermuda.) The "gentleman planters" who came to Jamestown prided themselves on their knowledge of literature and their ability to write beautifully. So it is that in the midst of describing his first visit to Powhatan, John Smith includes two lines of poetry translated into English from the Latin of the ancient Roman poet Lucretius.

All of the John Smith chapters are drawn from his writing, though I have sometimes modernized the spelling, changed the punctuation, or paraphrased. Every event that happens in these chapters can be found in his writings or in the accounts of others then in Jamestown, including Smith's adversary Master Edward Maria Wingfield.

Smith wrote several different accounts of the first year in Jamestown, including *A True Relation of Such Occurrences and Accidents of Noate as Hath Happened in Virginia* (1608) and *The Generall Historie of Virginia, the Somer Isles, and New England* (1623). I have used all of them as sources. Although Smith wrote most of his accounts in third person, referring to himself as "Smith," or "Captain Smith," I have chosen to put all of his chapters in the first-person voice of *A True Relation.* I also open each chapter with a relevant quote from a writer of his time.

As well as they wrote, some of the colonists' writing is a little difficult for us to understand today. Some of the words we use now had different meanings four hundred years ago. *Planter,* for example, means "colonist," while *discover* means "to explore." There are also some words that have totally vanished from modern English, such as *watchet* and *woosel.* Here is a selected glossary.

adays (adv.): by day
Admiral (n.): flagship, or the commander of the flagship
admire (v.): wonder about
ado (n.): excitement
adventure (v.): to explore
adventurer (n.): explorer or investor
alarum (n.): warning or cry of alarm
ambuscado (n.): ambush
barricado (n.): fortification
barrico (n.): keg or barrel
bastinado (n.): cudgel
bent (v.): aimed
bloody flux (n.): dysentery
bought (n.): river bend
bravery (n.): fine attire
break with (v.): tell or divulge to
bruit (n.): loud noise or clamor
burthen (n.): burden
cape merchant (n.): storehouse manager
card or **cart** (n.): chart or map
cautelous (adv.): cautious

champion (n.): open, flat country

check (n.): a reprimand

chicqueenes (n.): English spelling of the Italian word "zecchini," which were Venetian coins made of gold

chirugeon (n.): surgeon or doctor

conceit (v.): to think or imagine; or a plan

conceit (n.): a plan

contrive (v.): to design

corn (n.): originally, wheat, or any grain used for human food

discover (v.): to explore

doth (v.): does

doubt (v.): to fear

dryfats (n.): storage

environ (v.): surround

exception (n.): criticism

falchion (n.): sword

famous (adj.): fair or beautiful, excellent

flight shot (n.): an arrow shot

for that: because

garboil (n.): contention or argument

goodly (adj.): excellent

green wound (n.): flesh wound

grudging (v.): complaining

hap (n.): a happening, an occurrence

happy (adj.): lucky

height (n.): latitude on a map or chart

hie (v.): to hasten or hurry

hollow (n.): a howl

howbeit: although

humorist (n.): an impulsive person, ruled by his humors or moods

impale (v.): to fence in, to stockade

in fine: in the end, eventually

jealous (adj.): suspicious; also jealous in modern sense

lay by the heels: to imprison or put in irons

lugged (v.): burdened or encumbered

maintain (v.): to defend

mariner (n.): an experienced seaman, above a common sailor

marish (n.): marsh

match (n.): the fuse of a musket

meadow (n.): a low marsh

methinks (v.): I think, I believe

middest (adj.) midst, midmost, middle

misdoubt (v.): to disbelieve

murrey (adj.): purplish-red color

natural (n.): native person

offer (v.): attempt, try to

pace (n.): a passage through woods between bogs

pallisado (n.): a defensive wall or palisade

patent (n.): a charter or legal document issued by the king of England granting permission to establish a settlement in the New World

pennywhittle (n.): a small knife

piece (n.): gun

plant (v.): to establish a settlement or colony

planter (n.): a colonist or settler

popham side (n.): north or north bank of a river (From the fact that "Virginia," as the English called the East Coast, was divided between two British joint-stock companies. These were the Plymouth Company to the north, the area now known as New England, headed by Lord Popham, and the London Company to the south, headed by Lord Salisbury.)

presently (adv.): quickly

pretend (v.): to intend

prevent (v.): anticipate

privates (n.): favorites or close friends

privities (n.): one's private parts

pumpion (n.): pumpkin

putchamin (n.): persimmon

relade (v.): reload

resolution (n.): decision

Salisbury side (n.): south or south bank of a river

salvage (n.): native person, savage

season (v.): to grow accustomed to; used to describe the "seasoning" of the colonists, the period when many died as they tried to adapt to Virginia throughout the seasons

scape (n.): escape

shamefast (adj.): modest

so that: as long as

sound (n.): swoon

stay (v.): to delay, to defer

still (adv.): always

subtle (adj.): cunning, sneaky

target (n.): a light, round shield

taxed (v.): urged or ordered

temporize (v.): to negotiate, "wheel and deal"

touchwood (n.): tinder

treat (v.): to negotiate

trencher (n.): a platter of wood or metal

trial (n.): investigation

trucking (n.): trading
Tuftaffaty (adj.): finely dressed
tug (v.): to lug off or carry
victual (n.): food
want (n.): lack
watchet (adj.): sky-blue color
wheat (n.): Indian corn or any food grain
woosel (n.): blackbird

Powhatan Language

The language spoken by Pocahontas and her people is today referred to as Powhatan. It is an Algonquin language closely related to other Indian languages of the East Coast such as Lenape, Wampanoag, Mohegan, and Abenaki. Sadly, much of the Powhatan language has been lost, and it has not been in regular use for two centuries. Word lists were made by such people as John Smith and other colonists during the seventeenth century. A number of those words have, in slightly different form, entered the English language and are not recognized by most people as derived from Powhatan words. These include *arakun,* which became "raccoon"; *apone* or *ponepope,* which became "corn pone"; *muscascus,* which became "muskrat"; and, it seems, even *waugh,* which became "wow."

I have also included a list of the names of some places and actual Powhatan people of this period who appear in this book.

SELECTED WORDS

accowpret: shears
Ahone: creator and chief deity of the Powhatan world
amosens: daughter
apasoum: opossum

apone: cornbread

apooke: tobacco

arakun: raccoon; literally, "the one who scratches with his hands"

assapanick: flying squirrel

attasskuss: reed, water weed

attawp: bow

attone: arrow

aumoughhogh: shield

case: how many?

Cattapeuk: spring

chammy: a close friend

chepsin: land or earth

Cohattayough: summer

Cohonk: winter, probably from the sound of geese calling

copotone: sturgeon

crenepo: woman

hatto: small village

Huskanaw: rite of passage ceremony for boys

ka: what

kator: truly

kekaten: to tell

kekughes: life

Kefgawes: sun

kwiokosuk: minor deities

mache: now, at present

macokos: gourd

Mamanatowic: paramount chief

mangoi: large or great

Manguahaian: Great Bear or the Big Dipper constellation

maracocks: passion fruit

maraowanchesso: boy

marrapough: enemy

maskapow: worst enemy

matah: bad

matchcore: skin or garment

matchqueon: stone dust sprinkled onto body paint

mattasin: copper; literally, "red stone"

mattoume: large cane grass

mawchick chammay: best of friends

messamines: fox grape

mockasin: shoe

monacock: batonlike weapon, a wooden "sword"

mowchick: I

musquaspenne: bloodroot, dried root used as medicine or
    dye

muscascus: muskrat

musses: firewood, pieces of wood

nechaun: child (my child)

neheigh: to dwell

nemarough: man

nepawweshowgh: moon

Nepinough: season of corn forming ears

nettoppew: friend (my friend)

noughmass: fish

ocoughtanamins: chokecherry

Okeus: stern god who governs human affairs on earth

osies: heavens

pamesack: knife

pausarowmena: a dish made from boiled corn and beans;
    succotash

pawcorance: an altar stone

pawpecone: flute

pemmenaw: thread made of grass fibers

pokatawe: fire
poketawes: corn
ponepope: cornbread or corn pone
Popanow: winter
puccahiccora: drink made from hickory nuts
puccoon: skin paint made from various plants such as bloodroot; literally "blood"
pummahumps: star; **pummahumpal:** stars
pungwough: powdered ashes of corn cobs, used as a seasoning
putchamins: persimmon
quintans: canoe; **quintansuk:** canoes
quiyoughsokuk: priest, also a term for a minor deity; literally means "upright ones" or "just ones"
rawcomenes: gooseberry
rawcosowgh: day
rawrenock (roanoke): white-shell beads
righcomoughes: death
sacahocan: picture writing
sawwehone: blood
shacquohocan: a stone
suckahanna: water
tamehakan: tomahawk; literally, "chopper"
Taquitock: autumn
Tassantassa: newcomer or outsiders; **Tassantassuk:** outsiders
tawnor: where
tockahack: pickax
tockawhough: green arrow arum, tuckahoe
tomahak: ax
toppquough: night
tussan: bed
ussawassin: iron, silver, brass; literally, "yellow stone"

ustatahamen: hominy

uttapitchewayne: you lie

utteke: you go

vetchunquoyes: bobcat

wassacan: something that tastes spicy

waugh: Powhatan word to express wonder, pronounced "wow!"

weanok: sassafras

weghshaughes: flesh or meat

werowance: chief of a village; literally, "he is wealthy"

werowansqua: female chief

wighwhip: quickly

wingapo: hello; literally, "good man"

wisakon or **wighsakun:** medicine in general or a specific medicine made for "hurts and diseases" from milkweed

yihacan: house

yowo: this

yowrough: far, far away

PHRASES

Casa cunncack, peya quagh acquintan uttasantasough?
In how many days will there come here any more English ships?

Ka katorawincs yowo?
What do you call this?

Kator neheigh mattagh neer uttapitchewayne.
Truly he is there, I do not lie.

Kekaten Pokahontas patiaquagh ningh tanks manotyens neer mowchick rawrenock audowgh.
Bid Pokohontas bring here two little baskets, and I will give her white beads for a necklace.

Mache, neheigh yowrough, Orapaks.
Now he lives far away at Orapaks.
Mowchick woyawgh tawgh noetragh kaquere mecher?
I am very hungry, what shall I eat?
Spaughtynere keragh werowance Mawmarinough kekaten wawgh.
Run you to the werowance Mawmarynough and bid him come here.
Tawnor neheigh Powhatan?
Where lives Powhatan?
Uttapitchewayne anpechitchs nehawper werowocomoco.
You lie, he stays at Werowocomoco.
Utteke, e peya weyack wighwhip.
You go, and come again quickly.

NUMBERS

necut: one
ningh: two
nuss: three
yowgh: four
paranske: five
comotinch: six
toppawass: seven
nusswash: eight
kekatawgh: nine
kaskeke: ten

ninghsapooeksku: twenty
nussapooeksku: thirty
yowghapooeksku: forty
parankestasspooesku: fifty
comotinchtasspooesku: sixty

toppawasstasspooesku: seventy
nusswashtasspooesku: eighty
kekatawghtasspooesku: ninety
necuttoughtysinough: one hundred
necuttweunquaough: one thousand

PLACE NAMES

Chesepiock: Chesapeake Bay
Chickahominy: name of a river and also the Native people to the north of the Powhatans, not part of Powhatan's alliance
Kecoughtan: village at the head of the Chesapeake Bay
Paspahegh: Powhatan village on whose hunting lands Jamestown is built
Powhatan: principal village of the Powhatans upriver on the "James River," near the falls, where the werowance is one of Powhatan's sons
Rasawrack: literally, "in between" or "at the fork"; hunting camp where Smith is taken; also the name of the chief town of the Monacans
Werowocomoco: Powhatan's town, about fifteen miles north of Jamestown

NATIVE PEOPLE

Amocis: Powhatan man sent to observe the English
Naukaquawis: Pocahontas's brother
Nauiraus: Appamattuck man who guides Smith
Opechancanough: youngest half brother of Powhatan
Opitchapam: Younger, lame brother of Powhatan
Opposunoquonuske: weroansqua of the Appamattucks
Pocahontas/Matoaka/Amonute: favorite daughter of Powhatan

Powhatan/Wahunsonacock: Mamanatowic (paramount chief) of the Powhatan people
Rawhunt: elderly aide to Powhatan
Uttomatomakkin: Powhatan priest
Wowinchopunck: werowance of Paspahegh

A Note on the Stories of Pocahontas

I have tried to set the tone for each of the chapters by beginning them, in the case of John Smith, with a quote taken from a writer of the period, and, in the case of Pocahontas, with a Powhatan story. It is easy to indicate the sources of those quotes from the English (and one Spanish) chroniclers of the early seventeeth century. But where did I find the Powhatan stories?

I have reconstructed a series of tales by working from a combination of written documents, oral tradition, and intuition. John Smith's voluminous writings, of course, provide one source of such information, since he often describes Powhatan Indian customs and traditions with some accuracy—despite the fact that his interpretations are sometimes wrong. But other writers of the period also provide insights into Powhatan storytelling.

The History of Travel into Virginia Brittania was completed by William Strachey in 1612. It then reposed in manuscript form in the British Library for 237 years before being published in 1849 by the Hakluyt Society. In Chapter 7 of that volume can be found a relatively detailed telling of the Great Hare creation story, as it was related to Captain Samuel Argall by Henry Spelman, a teenage English boy who had been sent to live among the Indians and learn their language. (Spelman became a friend of Pocahontas's, and she saved his life on at least one occasion.) Certain other stories, which I have either read or heard in fragments, I have tried to reconstruct, keeping in mind the structure of Algonquin languages and the Powhatan worldview.

Two of the stories I attribute to the Powhatan people in this work of fiction are stories that, for a number of reasons, I believe were part of the Powhatan traditional canon of tales. These stories were known among Algonquin nations to the north and south of the Powhatans, and certain stories—such as that of the Great Bear or of Raccoon and his black mask—appear to have been almost universally known among the many Algonquin peoples. We come by stories in many ways—by listening to elders, by reading, by watching the natural world, and by hearing them on the wind. More than once I have told a tale that I thought had come to me purely from my imagination, only to find it was, indeed, a traditional story.

In short, all of the tellings in this book are in my own words, but they are firmly based on Powhatan and eastern Algonquin traditions.

A Note on Sources,
Hearing More than One Side...

The writing of this novel required a great deal of research and thought over many years. I have long been interested in the story of the Jamestown Colony and its impact on the lives of the Powhatan peoples, who both resisted and assisted those frequently wrongheaded first colonists. The real stories of John Smith and Pocahontas have seldom been fully told, much as they are a part of the popular imagination—even more since the highly distorted Disney movie a few years ago. To tell this story well, I thought, more than one voice and more than one point of view would be needed.

I then chose to look through the eyes of both the original Americans and the newcomers from England. I needed to see the same events from a European perspective at one moment and from an Indian one at the next. I found myself thankful for having studied the Elizabethan period while an undergraduate at Cornell University and having maintained an interest in the poetry and drama of the early seventeenth century (including teaching and producing the plays of Shakespeare in Ghana, West Africa, where I was a volunteer teacher from 1966 to 1969). The many English chroniclers who wrote so well and so much about this period from firsthand knowledge of the events were much like Shakespeare in their love for and their intoxication with the English language. There is real music in the turns of phrase to be found in the journals of John Smith, the observations of George Percy and Gabriell Archer, and even in Edward Maria Wingfield's self-serving *A Discourse of Virginia*. For anyone wishing to gain a sense of that period as described by such chroniclers, I highly recommend Edward Wright Haile's marvelous 1998 compilation, *Jamestown Narratives: Eyewitness Accounts of the Virginia Colony*. Interested readers might then move on to Philip L. Barbour's quite amazing three-volume set, *The Complete Works of Captain John Smith*.

Virginia has an incredibly rich history. Regular summer trips to visit my great-uncle Orvis Dunham in Warm Springs, Virginia, were an important part of my childhood and first sparked my interest in Jamestown. Back then, though, half a century ago, there was much less to see at Jamestown than there is now. The fifteen-hundred-acre island, which became part of the Colonial National Historical Park in 1933, is largely deserted, and the loop road that runs through the island passes through forests and marshes that look much as they did five centuries ago. However, there is now a National Parks Service visitors' center that shows a fine film about the hardships of the first years of Jamestown.

It was long thought that the James River, which shifted its banks over the centuries, had washed away all that remained of Jamestown. However, in the late 1980s, archaeologists found the site of the Jamestown settlement and, in 1996, the footprint of the first fort. Although a few memorials stand on the island (including awful statues of a massively heroic John Smith and a rather pathetic Pocahontas dressed like a Plains Indian), no one lives there today and a visitor can easily find enough solitude to imagine what it was like when those first three ships swam into view.

To see those three ships, or at least accurate, seaworthy replicas of them, one only needs to drive back across the narrow bridge from Jamestown Island to visit the state-run living history museum of Jamestown Settlement. Tied up to the pier are brightly painted, fully functioning reproductions of the 116-foot-long *Susan Constant,* the *Godspeed,* and the *Discovery* (which is about the size of a school bus). The accurate (though, of course, sanitized) details of the stockaded fort and re-created Powhatan Indian village are further brought to life by the well-informed people who work there, dressed in the clothing of the period and engaged in the everyday activities of the first decades of the settlement. A number of the surviving tribal nations of Virginia take an active part in the Jamestown Settlement Museum, not only as reenactors, but also in the annual Virginia Indian Heritage Festival, which takes place there every June and is cosponsored by the Virginia Indian Council. For more information and a listing of the many special events at Jamestown Settlement, visit its Web site at www.nps.gov/colo or call (757) 229-1607.

Among my most important scholarly resources for the Powhatan side of the story were the works of Helen C. Rountree, whose studies of the coastal peoples of Virginia have rightly been called a model of historical ethnology. The respect she enjoys among contemporary Native Americans of that region is deeply deserved. Her 1989 book, *The Powhatan Indians of Virginia: Their Traditional Culture,* is only one of her many invaluable contributions.

I was also assisted by a number of Native people who pointed me in the right direction on more occasions than one. Prominent among those who helped me see the world through Powhatan eyes are Jack Forbes and my dear friends Powhatan Eagle and his sister Matoaka Little Eagle. It has been said that the Powhatan language is extinct, but it is also true that it has probably supplied more "loan words" to the English language than any other American Indian tongue. The most prominent lists of Powhatan words and phrases are those of John Smith from his *Map of Virginia* (1612) and William Strachey in *The History of Travel* (completed in 1612, first published in 1849), which contain about a thousand entries.

Further, as a member of the great Algonquin language family, the structure and many of the actual words in Powhatan (such as the words to count from one to ten) are virtually the same as in my own Abenaki language. Although I have my Powhatan characters speaking in English (with occasional words in Powhatan), I have tried to "think Algonquin" in each of the chapters devoted to the point of view of Pocahontas and then translate that thought into English.

I did something very similar in writing the John Smith chapters. To begin with (as my editor, Paula Wiseman, and the long-suffering members of my writing group know all too well), I not only used one of John Smith's own frequent devices—writing about himself in the third person—in my first draft of the book, I also copied the style and language of Smith's period, often borrowing whole sentences from Smith's own written accounts. The result was, though perhaps somewhat authentic, also certainly somewhat frustrating to read without footnotes. In my final revision, I changed these chapters to first-person narrative and simplified the language so that it conformed more (but not completely) to modern English.

You'll note, though, in my novel that John Smith still occasionally insists on referring to himself in the third person.

In seeing things from the Native American side, I have to admit that my Ph.D. in comparative literature was much less helpful than the last four decades I have spent deepening my knowledge of my own American Indian heritage by listening to and spending time with the many friends, fellow storytellers, and elders in the Native American community who have shared and continue to share so much with me, with such great generosity.

I often mention that one of the wisest things I was ever taught—and taught more than once—by Native elders is that all of us have two ears. One of the reasons for that, I was told by such teachers as Swift Eagle and Harold Tantaquidgeon, was that our Creator wished us to remember that there are two sides to every story. I hope that I have listened well enough to help my readers hear the two quite distinct sides to this tale of the first year of Jamestown Settlement.

Selected Bibliography

Barbour, Philip L., ed. *The Complete Works of Captain John Smith, Volumes I–III.* Chapel Hill, N.C.: University of North Carolina Press, 1986.

Doherty, Kieran. *To Conquer Is to Live: The Life of Captain John Smith of Jamestown.* Breckenridge, Colo.: Twenty-First Century Books, 2001.

Feest, Christian F. *The Powhatan Tribes.* New York: Chelsea House Publishers, 1990.

Haile, Edward Wright, ed. *Jamestown Narratives: Eyewitness Accounts of the Virginia Colony.* Champlain, Va.: RoundHouse, 1998.

Hume, Ivor Noel. *The Virginia Adventure: Roanoke to James Towne: An Archaeological and Historical Odyssey.* Charlottesville, Va.: University Press of Virginia, 1994.

Kupperman, Karen Ordahl, ed. *Captain John Smith: A Select Edition of His Writings.* Chapel Hill, N.C.: University of North Carolina Press, 1988.

Rountree, Helen C. *Pocahontas's People: The Powhatan Indians of Virginia through Four Centuries.* Norman, Okla.: University of Oklahoma Press, 1990.

Rountree, Helen C. *The Powhatan Indians of Virginia: Their Traditional Culture.* Norman, Okla.: University of Oklahoma Press, 1989.

Smith, Julian. *Virginia Handbook.* Emeryville, Calif.: Moon Travel Handbooks/Avalon Travel Publishing, 1999.